Mystery of White Horse Lake

Best wishes!
Frances Powell

Frances Powell

Other novels by Frances Powell

The Bodyguard

A Ballysea Mystery Series:

The O'Brien

A Bad Wind Blowing

The O'Brien: The Untold Story

Cover Design by: Jo Stallings

Copyright 2017 Frances Powell

ISBN 978-1-48359-747-8

Preface

I stood silently at the window, watching and waiting.

After everyone else had gone to bed, I kept watch over the still waters of the lake, as I had every night this entire year. I worried about the small children upstairs snug in their beds, mindless of the danger. I knew he would come. I had been forewarned by the Sidhe, the fairies who called these mountains their home, that they had summoned their emissary of death. He appeared every seven years without fail. This year marked seven years since his last appearance and the horror left in his wake. But when would he come and who was he coming for?

It was on this moonlit night in early winter when the phantom white stallion arose from the dark waters of Pola Capall Lake. Shaking the water from his long, flowing mane, he cast his eyes upward towards the castle and stared with blazing eyes at the window where I stood.

Raising his foreleg at the water's edge, he pawed the earth three times. Then, rearing up on his hind legs, the majestic beast turned and raced across the mirror-like waters of the lake. His message was clear. Death would come to claim another soul within three days.

Chapter 1

I came to Castle Chonamara, wedged between the rugged, wild Connemara Mountains and the still waters of Pola Capall Lake as a young girl of twelve, nearly fifty years ago. Then I was but a lowly housemaid to the first owners of the castle. After many years and as many owners, I had finally risen to the position of housekeeper.

When the castle was completed in 1867, some twenty years after the devastating potato crop failures and the famine, it meant work and hope for those in the surrounding area who remained. It was only a year after the quietness of the wilderness was disturbed by the building of the castle that the phantom white horse first appeared.

At first no one knew why he had come, but it later became apparent that the castle had been built on ground sacred to the Sidhe, fairies that inhabited this part of Ireland. Using an ancient curse, they were able to summon the White Horse once every seven years to punish anyone who dared disturb the tranquility of their valley. Whatever the reason, the legend of the White Horse that brought death and tragedy to those living in the castle grew among all who lived in these mountains.

The scullery maid, Maeve, was the first to see the eerie shape of the stallion one winter night under a waning moon, as it pawed the earth on the castle drive before turning and seeming to glide across the still waters of the lake before diving deep into its depths. Like me, Maeve was a local village girl, but unlike Maeve, I had been educated. By that I mean I could read and write English, thanks to the insistence of my Mam who once worked as a governess for a wealthy family in England before marrying my Da. Maeve was a hard worker, but like many superstitious locals she believed in the fairies and local legends. Until that night, I

4

always thought of the legend of the fairies as children's stories. Perhaps, the rest of the staff felt the same way and maybe that's why they scoffed when she told them what she had seen. I think I was the only one who believed Maeve. For you see I, and I alone, had witnessed the look of sheer terror on her face that moonlit winter night when she came back into the kitchen after emptying the scraps from dinner.

I was only a young child of thirteen years, but I shall never forget the very next day when little Master Jeromy, the youngest of the Earl's seven children, was taken from us. He was a lively little boy with the sweetest disposition and the face of an angel, with engaging blue eyes and beautiful silky blond ringlets. Never one to hold with class distinction, he was happy to join in the games with the estate manager, Dan Mooney's rowdy brood. It was during these games tragedy struck. The freezing cold winter weather had frozen over a small corner of the lake and the children had been skating on it for days. The depth of the ice was supposed to be checked daily by Mr. Mooney to insure the safety of the children, but on that tragic day he had come home drunk the night before, to abuse his wife and children again and lay abed until after the children left to skate. It had been safe enough to hold his rather rotund frame the day before, so surely it would still be safe enough to hold a lean lad of seven years. That was what he thought, as he dozed in his bed nursing his hangover, but in the end, it was not.

He was gone before anyone could do anything. The other children raised the alarm and Mr. Mooney jumped out of bed half-dressed and tried desperately to break the ice to free the still-living child, but it was to no avail and he disappeared from sight under the dark waters. They found him hours later, still trapped under the ice, staring up at the sky with his beautiful blue eyes wide-open looking towards heaven where he had been taken way too soon.

His limp little body was carried in the arms of his grieving father slowly up the front steps of the castle. We all stood lined up at the door with our heads bowed and tears streaming from our eyes. It was that fond of the wee child we all were. Old Mrs. Monahan came as quickly as her aging legs could carry her. It would be her task to dress young Jeromy for the laying out. Thank goodness the old days of the shroud had passed and at least his family would spend their final days with their beloved child dressed as he would have been in life.

The housekeeper, Mrs. Brown, looped white crepe tied with a white ribbon upon the door so any callers would know a child had died and the family was in mourning. Despite the cold weather and snow showers, the front door was left ajar to allow family and all those calling to offer their sympathy without ringing the bell.

Because of my ability to write, I was asked to take on the duty of sending out the funeral invitations. I had never heard of such a thing. In our village, a death usually brought everyone out to pay their respects, but I was told by Mrs. Brown it was always done in society. After getting the list of people to invite from Mrs. Brown, I set to work. I knew it was going to be a late night since they needed to be sent out in the morning. I was given a box of small white notepaper with a wide black border and a list of names and instructions as to what to write. And so I began my duty, working long into the night by lamplight.

"You and your family are respectfully invited to attend the funeral of Master Jeromy Johnson, from Chonamara Castle on Wednesday, 21st of December, at 11 o'clock Burial to follow in the Family Mausoleum on the grounds."

In the morning, Mrs. Brown found me fast asleep with my head resting on my crossed arms; still sitting slumped over at the desk. My work done, the kindly, old housekeeper sent me to my bed in the servant's quarters.

After the funeral, the kitchen was kept busy cooking for the many visitors who came from far and wide to pay their respects to the grieving family, It would be a long six months of mourning as the castle and estate grew as quiet as little Jeremy in his crypt.

All who worked at Castle Chonamara hoped the end of mourning and the return of summer would bring some semblance of normalcy to the castle and those who lived and worked there, but it was not to be. Our poor mistress could not shake the dark depression which held her in its grip since the White Horse had taken her youngest. It came as no surprise when Mrs. Brown announced to the staff over dinner that the family would be returning to London for the unforeseeable future. Everyone stopped eating and held their breath until Mrs. Brown announced that his Lordship had ordained that the entire staff be kept on at full pay. Each member was also given a week off to go visit their own families as a gift in remembrance of his dear, departed son, who had been treated with so much kind affection by the castle staff.

I was glad to get away from the castle when my turn came to spend a week with my family. It was so quiet without the family in residence and with little to do; the days seem to go on forever. I was rewarded for my assistance in writing the funeral invitations with an extra pound in my pay packet. This was what I would normally earn for a full month of labor. With that in hand, I went home to my family with the intention of passing it on to my mother to help with the family expenses. With four younger brothers to feed and clothe there was always the need for extra money.

When I returned to the castle a week later, I wasn't surprised to find Mr. Mooney had been discharged and he and his family were gone. Unfortunately, there was more sad news. Our kind owner had sent word the castle was to be sold. As much as he loved the dream home he had built for his family, neither he nor his wife could face returning and having to look daily at the lake which had taken their youngest child. The news quickly spread among those who lived in the rural county for whom the master had done so much since beginning work on the castle and the surrounding estate. In addition to employing so many locals to work inside the massive castle there was an equal amount hired to maintain the estate and its grounds. His charitable gifts to the people in this rural county were to leave a lasting impression on the people here. Long after he had gone to his grave, his name was still being spoken with great respect by all who had benefited from his kindness.

It wasn't long after this that Maeve also left the castle never to return. She had begun to have some type of fits during which she would stare glassy-eyed and chant over and over in a sing-song voice,

"I didn't come for the lad,

I came for Mooney, that evil man.

The White Horse only takes the bad.

It was never the fairies plan."

There were many who didn't take notice of this, but I later grew to understand the chant's meaning. As time went on, the White Stallion only seemed to bring death to those the Sidhe deemed unworthy to walk on their sacred grounds.

Chapter 2

The years passed quietly and I had just reached my twentieth birthday in 1875, when he came again. Things had been turned upside down five years ago when the new owners moved into the castle. After almost two years of just the odd hunting party or prospective buyer coming to spend a brief period of time at the estate, having to deal with this new family was quite grueling.

The new family in residence consisted of Lord Andrew Parker and his wife Lady Isabelle Parker and their two nearly grown children. They had come across from Scotland after some type of scandal involving their son, James. Stories abound around the servants' quarters regarding his dalliance with the daughter of the owner of an adjoining estate in Scotland that had ended in her disgrace. Within months of their taking up residence, these rumors were substantiated. Not one of the pretty maids working within the castle walls was safe from his unwelcome advances.

The new owner, himself, was the complete opposite of our beloved former owner. Gone was the benevolent treatment of those who worked within the castle and on the surrounding estate. The beautiful chapel built by the Earl for his devote Catholic family and all locals who desired to worship there was padlocked shut. The school built for the local children closed soon after, as Lord Parker felt educating the poor was a waste of time and good money. There were staff cuts causing everyone to work longer hours for less pay. Those first to go were any of the young maids who dared to complain of his son's misconduct towards them. With few other options for employment in the mountains, we had little choice but to tolerate the new working conditions.

If there was one redeeming factor of this blight on the castle brought by Lord Parker, it was his good wife, Lady Parker. The kind mistress, while appearing to acquiesce to the actions of her husband in his presence, was very different when he and their son traveled to London pursuing their political ambitions. It was as if the cloak of darkness was lifted from the castle during those months when the two men, who were so much alike, were absent. The heavy drapes were pulled back allowing the sunshine to once again stream through the high windows, which faced the glistening waters of the lake. The sweet scent of flowers once again drifted through the main floor rooms as Lady Parker and her shy daughter, Amelia, arranged the large ornate vase of flowers on the round mahogany table below the grand staircase in the entrance hall.

Amelia was a favorite among the staff. The quiet, petite girl often stopped by the ground floors to visit with me and the rest of the staff when her father and brother were away. Other than her mother for company, Amelia had no other female companionship and was lonely. Lady Parker aware of her daughter's intelligence tried without success to convince her husband to allow her only daughter to attend boarding school in England where she would not only have opportunities to expand her knowledge but also female companionship.

It was on one particularly warm spring day while I was serving the mistress her tea in the garden when she asked me to sit, then asked, "Cathleen, may I ask you something rather personal?"

Looking around to be certain Mrs. Brown, the housekeeper, wasn't in sight, I slipped quickly onto the garden bench opposite her and replied, "Yes ma'am, of course. What is it you wish to know?"

Putting her teacup down, she said, "I can't help but notice that you are somewhat different from the rest of the staff employed here."

Sighing and beginning to twist her lace handkerchief in her dainty hands, she continued, "I'm sorry. I'm not explaining this very well. What I'm trying to say is, you have obviously been educated and instructed in the proper deportment for a young lady. Am I correct in my assumption?'

Shyly lowering my gaze, I replied softly, "Yes Lady Parker. My mother is English and had worked for a well-to-do family in England as governess to their children before marrying my father and moving here. She is the one who has taught me as well as my brothers."

"You read and write English?"

"Yes ma'am. I love to read. The old Earl always allowed me to borrow books from the library to read in my off hours and during the worse of the winter I would read out loud after dinner to the other staff. They seemed to enjoy the stories as much as I did."

Setting her cup down and rising to her feet, Lady Parker smiled as she said, "Then it's settled. I would like you to be lady's maid to my daughter. She has reached the age when she should have her own maid and I'm sure even my husband can't object to that. With this new position, you will of course have an increase in your wages as well as access to the library when desired. Will that be agreeable to you?"

Quickly jumping to my feet the minute Lady Parker rose from her seat, I stood with my mouth open staring at her kind, smiling face. It was a few minutes before I could find my voice and reply, "Yes ma'am. I would like that very much. Thank you."

"Very good, I will speak to Mrs. Brown immediately and inform my daughter you have accepted the position. She will be thrilled," said Lady Parker as she lifted her long skirts and swept across the freshly manicured lawn towards the steps and the open front door.

I scurried back to the kitchen with the tea tray just as Lady Parker summoned Mrs. Brown to her study. It wasn't long before a fuming Mrs. Brown stormed back into the kitchen and pointed at me as she announced gruffly for all the staff to hear, "Her ladyship over there will be moving upstairs as lady's maid to Mistress Amelia. It would appear Miss Cullen here has risen above her station."

At least most of the other servants were pleased with my good fortune, but there were some who I could tell were not. I couldn't really blame them because I knew it would mean more work for the other maids who would have to take on the duties vacated by me.

I had been lady's maid to Mistress Amelia for a little over a month when the fairies first appeared. We had been in the garden gathering flowers for the arrangements she and her mother changed almost daily during the summer. The day suddenly turned chilly and I had run into the castle to fetch a shawl for my mistress. I came back to find her peering into the flowering bushes on the side of the flower bed.

"Miss Amelia, whatever are you doing? You'll get your lovely frock dirty."

Spreading the branches apart, Amelia looked back over her shoulder and called to me, "Come quick, Cathleen. Can you see them?"

Thinking she had seen one of the many beautiful birds that lived in the garden, I moved closer and asked, "Is it one of your favorite little Robins?"

"Shhh...Can you hear them talking?"

"No, hear who?" I asked moving closer and looking into Amelia's wide eyes.

Fearing she was having some type of fit, I quickly grabbed her arm and propelled her to a seat in the shade. Amelia stared wide-eyed at me and said, "They said to tell you to be careful because you are in danger but not to worry; you will be protected."

20

"Are you feeling alright Miss? Who are you talking about?

Amelia was quiet for just a minute and then whispered, "I had seen them before but told no one. I went to the library and I read about them."

"Read about whom?" I asked.

"The Sidhe, of course. The books said they are angels who fell to earth before humans resided on the land and water. I knew it was them. They were very small and dressed in green tunics. I have been leaving some bits of the cakes from our teas to thank them for allowing the garden to grow and flourish. That is what the books said the Irish people do. The Sidhe are the ones who make this garden so beautiful."

"Did they tell you what danger and who is going to protect me?" I asked.

"I don't know Cathleen. They didn't say but they were very insistent you would be protected. I thought at first they were some type of small birds until I saw their tiny faces. It was then I realized they were the Sidhe."

Taking her hands in mine, I looked seriously into Amelia's eyes and whispered, "I really think we should keep this a secret between us."

Suddenly realizing what her domineering father and her bully of a brother would say if she mentioned what she had seen and heard Amelia began slowly nodding her head. Her father already berated his daughter every time the opportunity arose. I dreaded to think what he would do if she told anyone she had heard and seen what I could only speculate were the fairies of local legend, said to protect these sacred mountains.

With the secret safe between us, we gathered up the flowers we had picked and strolled quietly out of the gardens and along the path by the lake to the castle beyond. We had just begun to climb the wide, white marble steps when her brother, James, came bounding down the steps heading for the stables. As he passed by very close to my side, I felt the pressure of his hand as it brushed my breast through my thin summer frock. This wasn't the first time I had been subjected to Master James' unwanted attentions but it was the first time it was witnessed by anyone. As I raised my eyes to the open doorway, I witnessed his mother. Lady Parker, standing red-faced and open mouthed.

Waiting until Amelia was out of earshot, Lady Parker placed her hand gently on my arm and reassuring me said, "I am sorry Cathleen. I will speak to my son. He will not bother you again."

Just nodding, I placed the flowers we had picked in the garden on the hall table and followed Amelia upstairs to her suite and then to my small room beyond. As I changed for afternoon tea, I suddenly thought the fairies prediction had indeed come true. I was in danger from Master James but now thanks to his mother the threat would be removed. At least that was what I thought.

Chapter 3

Two weeks passed when a messenger brought word to the castle that my Da had been injured at work and my mother requested I be allowed to come home to see him and help her with my younger brothers so she could tend my father. Mrs. Brown received permission from Lady Parker and I quickly packed and began the hour walk to my small village, just east of the castle. I had just started to pass the far end of the lake when Master James walked out from the woods and blocked my path.

"My...my, now where are you going with your bag packed? Did my father give you your walking papers after you complained to my mother about me?"

I just lowered my gaze and shook my head from side-to-side.

"No? Well, I can tell you complaining to my mother will do you no good. Her words mean nothing here. She's just a decoration to be shown off on my father's arm and someone to keep this castle running while we're away," sneered James as he moved dangerously close.

As he reached for me, the wind began to pick up and the limbs on the trees began to bend and twist as an eerie sound filled the air. I was rooted to the spot unable to move. It was then that I saw him. He seemed to glide across the waters of the lake and silently moved directly behind Master James. I don't think he was aware of anything until it was too late. The massive white horse snorted loudly and began pawing the ground as he advanced on Master James, forcing him backwards towards the water's edge. Suddenly, the waters of the lake began churning and I watched horrified as the lake grass began wrapping itself around his feet and up his legs like slithering snakes and pulling him farther into the icy waters. For the first time, I saw something on his arrogant face I had never seen before. He wore a look of sheer terror as he reached his hands out to me for help. Finally able to move my feet, I tried desperately to reach his outstretched hands, but every time our hands touched the big stallion moved forward placing himself between me and James. By the time he finally moved away, Master James was gone. Staring into the eyes of the horse, I realized now what the fairies warning had meant. Within seconds the giant of a horse turned and was gone gliding across the lake before diving under its waters. It wasn't until later that I remembered it had been exactly seven years since the first sighting of the White Horse of the lake.

As I turned to run back to the castle, I saw Lady Parker and Miss Amelia coming slowly down the path towards me. What was I to tell them? Would they think me crazy like poor little Maeve if I told them about the White Horse?

Before I could say a word, Lady Parker wrapped her arms around me and whispered,

27

"I was watching from the garden and saw what my son was trying to do to you and I heard what he said about me. I also saw what happened. We will say no more about the White Horse and what happened here. My son was coming home after spending too much time in the pub, as usual, and slipped and fell into the lake and drowned. Amelia and I both saw you try to save him but it was too late. Now you go on and see your father. Stay a week. We'll be fine. Now hurry, I need to raise the alarm."

Hugging the good lady back, I grabbed my bag and left, as fast as I could, never looking back as I hurried for the safety of my childhood home.

Mother was standing looking out the half-door watching for me when I rounded the bend and entered the village. I watched as her smile turned to a frown as she rushed out the door and ran to meet me.

"Whatever is wrong child? You are as white as a ghost. Is it your father's accident that has you so upset?" asked my mother clasping me to her.

"Let's go inside mother and I will tell you the tragic news from the castle," I replied slipping my arm around my mother's waist as we entered our family home.

Our cottage, built those many years ago by my grandfather, was built of the stones from the surrounding fields and covered with a thatch roof. Like most of the worker's cottages our home consisted of one large room which served as our kitchen and sitting area and two smaller sleeping quarters. When I came home for the occasional visit, my mother would lay out a pallet of thick blankets in the evening and I would sleep on the floor by the fire. The only door to the cottage was a half door in the front. The half door remained open to allow light and fresh air in, even in the coldest of weather. I only remember it being closed when the summer rains or the winter snows blew their moisture into the cottage.

No sooner had mother entered the cottage, she immediately headed for the range and grabbed the kettle that was constantly left ready for tea. Mother kept the stove running with the peat from the bogs that Da or the boys cut and dried. It was our only source of heat and cooking fuel, like all of our neighbors.

Pointing to the bedroom she and my father shared she said, "Go in and see your father. He's been asking for you all morning. I'll bring the tea."

My father sat propped up against his pillows on the bed with his bandaged leg lying uncovered on top of the bedding. As I approached, he pulled his pipe from his mouth and smiled as he patted the bed, signaling me to sit beside him.

Carefully sitting, as to not brush against his swollen, bandaged leg, I leaned forward and placed a kiss on his unshaven cheek and asked, "How are you, Da? Does it pain you much?"

"Not anymore Cathleen. I am on the mend these last two days, thanks to your mother's fine nursing skills," he said as he smiled up at her as she entered the room with a tray and three cups of tea.

After passing out the tea, she said, "Now tell us the news from the castle."

Crossing my hands in my lap, I began reciting Lady Parker's version of the events leading up to Master James' death.

Shaking her head my mother said, "Poor Lady Parker. It's such a tragedy for her to lose her only son in such a manner because of the drink."

Being the sympathetic man he was, my father said, "Shouldn't you be with Lady Parker and Mistress Amelia in their time of sorrow?"

Shaking my head I replied, "No Da, I did offer but she said I was to take the whole week at home for trying to save Master James and to get over the shock of witnessing his death."

Nodding, as he placed his pipe back in his mouth he said, "You're a good girl, Cathleen. I'm very proud of you, my daughter."

I smiled but remained silent. I couldn't help but wonder what my parents, who didn't believe in the fairies or such things as curses, would say if they knew the truth.

The week went by all too quickly and the day had come for me to return to the castle. The day I left was the first day my father was out of the bed and walking about with the aid of his stick. The natural color had returned to his leg and all signs of infection were gone, thanks to my mother's knowledge of medicinal herbs.

After I packed my bag and bade goodbye to my younger brothers, I turned my attention to my parents. Hugging them tightly, I promised to come home as soon as I could get some time off and made them promise to send word if they needed me for anything. As I left, I took my mother's hand and slipped my last month's wage into it to help hold them over until my father could resume work. Hugging me tightly, she walked with me to the edge of the village and watched as I took the road going through the woods to the castle.

As I got closer to the castle my pace began to slow. I had no way of knowing what had transpired at the castle since Master James' death and the fear of the unknown now held me in its grip. I played out every scenario in my mind as I began the walk around the lake towards the castle. Was Lady Parker's story questioned? Would Lord Parker blame me for not saving his son? I was becoming more and more frantic with each step I took.

As I approached the front steps, Amelia ran flying out the front door and excitedly grabbed my hand almost pulling me the rest of the way inside the castle.

"I'm so glad you're back. Mother told me to keep watch and bring you to her as soon as you returned," said Amelia.

Out of breath I asked, "What has happened now? Is everything alright?"

Smiling Amelia said, "Mother will explain all."

I had no sooner slipped out of my coat than Amelia was propelling me through into the library. As I entered the room, Lady Parker looked up from her needlework and smiled as she patted the chair alongside her, signaling me to sit. I was surprised to see her looking so calm and serene so close to the death of her only son.

Before I had the chance to offer condolences from me and my family she reached over and taking my hand said, "I hope you found your father much improved."

Nodding, I replied, "Yes, he is now able to walk with his stick and thanks to my mother's nursing skills, all signs of infection are gone. But more important how are you?"

Patting my hand she replied, "I won't pretend that losing my son doesn't break my heart but you have to understand that I lost my sweet little boy years ago when his father first took an interest in him and began molding him in his own evil image. Now they are both gone, I believe our lives will be much improved."

For a moment I didn't quite comprehend what she was trying to tell me, and confused I asked, "Both?"

"Oh my dear, I am so sorry. I thought the news would have reached you in the village by now. You see, Lord Parker had a massive stroke when told of James' death and despite the doctor's best efforts, he died the next morning. I had the chapel re-opened and after a private funeral service, I had them interred there side-by-side."

Not sure how to respond, I simply replied, "I'm so sorry for your loss."

Patting my hand again, Lady Parker smiled and said, "Thank you my dear, but sadly I feel more relief than loss."

Continuing she said, "You will find I have made some changes this week while you've been away. The chapel is now open and I've arranged for a priest to conduct services on Sundays for anyone who wishes to attend. I also plan on re-opening the school, as soon as I can find a teacher, and that's why I wanted to speak with you as soon as you returned. I was wondering if your mother would consider taking the position. I would also wish to employ your father. I have been told he is an excellent gardener and as I have big plans for the gardens, I'm in need of a head gardener. It wouldn't be hard work for him. He would be directing the under-gardeners and working with me on the plans. They would both have a good wage and the boys could attend school and help around the castle, if they wish to earn extra pocket-money. Your parents would, of course, have the use of the Gardener's Cottage at no rent with its three bedrooms and indoor toilet, for as long as they live."

After her long speech, I just sat with my mouth hanging open. When I left my parent's home, I wasn't sure how they were going to get through the winter. This offer of employment was a godsend and I'm sure one they would both be eager to undertake. As for me, the thought of having my beloved family living just across the gardens from me was more than I could have ever wished for.

Not sure what my stunned reaction was to her proposition, Lady Parker asked hesitantly, "Does the idea not please you?"

"It sounds wonderful, but I will have to ask my parents, of course."

With that Lady Parker smiled and said, "Of course you must. I will arrange for Mr. Murphy to take you by carriage on the weekend and if they agree we can arrange a date convenient to them, and I will send some men and a cart to help them with the move."

Lady Parker reached over and squeezed my hand one last time as she rose from her chair and seemed to glide from the library. I stood transfixed for a few moments, until Amelia came to the door and holding out her hand to me said, "I am so glad your father is on the mend and I hope they will come and live here with us."

'Were you listening at the door again, Miss Amelia?" I asked with a twinkle in my eyes.

Smiling brightly, as she pulled me towards the stairs and the privacy of her rooms she replied,

"Of course I was, and I have much more to tell you!"

We spent the rest of the afternoon, until we were called for tea, talking about the changes which had occurred in the short time I had been away from the castle. I was surprised to hear that all the wealth in the family came from Lady Parker's inheritance and now that there were no male head-of-households, she had full control of her vast fortune. From what Amelia was saying, she fully intended spending it to improve the lives of everyone employed on the estate and this area of Connemara she had grown to love.

Over tea, Lady Parker laid out her plans for a walled garden and what she hoped my father could help her accomplish. My father had been head gardener of the large estate in England where my mother worked as governess before they wed. I had no doubt he could transform the garden into the magnificent walled garden she envisioned. The only thing left was to see if he and Mother would accept Lady Parker's offers of employment.

The rest of the week passed by quickly and true to her word, Lady Parker instructed Mr. Murphy to bring the carriage around to the front of the castle and drive me to my parent's home. The elder Mr. Murphy was in charge of the stables and was for the most-part grumpy. Today though, as we drove down the long drive from the castle, he seemed almost happy as he whistled a lively tune. I couldn't help but say, "Mr. Murphy, you seem very light-hearted today."

"Why yes Miss, and why wouldn't I be? I have more money in my wage packet and Saturdays and Sundays off to spend time with my family and to rest my weary bones."

Amelia had told me about her mother raising the pay of all the employees on the estate but I didn't understand how she could give Mr. Murphy off on the weekend when the horses

40

would need to be tended and she might need a driver, if she desired to go out in the carriage.

"But who will take care of the horses and drive Lady Parker, if you have those days off?" I asked.

"Well, that's the beauty of it. Our kind mistress has hired my eldest son to work with me and he will work the weekends. Not only will he be able to learn a trade, she is going to pay him while he is learning. She's a godsend our lady is."

I could only smile and reply, "Yes, she truly is Mr. Murphy."

Father was leaning on the half door of our cottage smoking his pipe when he spotted the carriage coming up the lane. As I stepped down from the carriage, he called into the cottage, "Mother, we have an unexpected guest."

Mother was wiping the flour from her hands onto her apron as she came out the door.

Pushing stray strands of hair away from her face she ran to meet me and anxiously asked, "What's happened Cathleen? We weren't expecting you home so soon. You haven't lost your position too have you?"

Hugging her tightly I said, "No Mother, everything is fine, but what do you mean by 'too'?"

"Come inside and let me put the kettle on and I'll tell you the news."

Turning at the door, she called to Mr. Murphy, "Can I offer you a cup of tea, Mr. Murphy?"

"No thank you, Mrs. Cullen. I have to attend to some shopping for the Missus. I'll be back in a couple hours to collect Miss Cathleen."

Waving goodbye, I called after him, "Thank you Mr. Murphy. I'll be ready."

Da was sitting in his chair by the fire still smoking his pipe when we entered the kitchen. I was shocked by his appearance. In the short week I'd been gone, he appeared to have aged ten years.

Mother quickly fixed the tea and nodded her head in the direction of the bedroom, indicating she wanted to speak with me out of earshot of my father. After we had settled down, she leaned forward and in a half-whisper explained, "Your Father has lost his position and he is worried. With no other work going around the village, we may be forced to move away."

As her eyes began to well up with tears, I quickly grabbed her shaking hands and explained the reason for my visit.

"Mother, Lady Parker has sent me to see you and Da about an offer she would like me to put to you. She wants to extend the castle gardens to include a walled garden, similar to the one Father created for the manor house where the two of you worked before you married. She wants Da to help with the planning and supervise the under-gardeners.

43

She also wants to re-open the school and wondered if you would consider coming to work there as the teacher. "

Knowing Lord Parker's mean and stingy reputation, Mother slowly shook her head and replied, "Your Father could never work for someone like his Lordship. I can't believe Lord Parker would even consider the offer, after all it was him who closed the school and he has no time for the gardens."

"I guess you haven't heard," I said slowly.

"Heard what, Cathleen?"

"Lord Parker doesn't make the decisions at the castle anymore. The shock of his son's death was too much for him. He had a stroke and died."

"No, we hadn't heard the news. I can't say he'll be missed but how will Lady Parker manage?" asked my mother.

Smiling now I said, "Lady Parker is doing quite well actually. It seems that she's the one who brought her wealth to the marriage and now with no surviving male she's in full control of her money and her destiny."

Rising from her chair, Mother crossed into the kitchen and pulled a stool out and sat at Father's feet. Reaching out and laying her hand upon his knee, she said, "Michael, we have had a job offer from Lady Parker."

Still staring into the open fire he replied, "And since when does Lady Parker do the hiring at the castle?"

Stepping forward and placing my hand on his shoulder I said, "Since her husband's death. She sent me here today to ask you if you would consider taking on the post of head gardener and help her to create a walled garden, like the one you did in England. You and mother would have the gardener's cottage for life."

I watched my father look from me to my mother as he asked her, "What say you, Mother?"

Reaching over and taking his rough hands in hers, she said, "It sounds like a godsend, Michael."

Hesitating for just a moment, I looked at both of them and continued, "There was one other thing she would like you to consider."

"What is that, my dear," asked Da.

"Lady Parker has reopened the chapel and arranged for a priest to conduct Sunday mass for all those who wish to attend and now she wants to start up the school again. The only thing stopping her is that she needs a teacher and she was hoping Mother would consider taking on the job."

Mother and Da exchanged looks until Father finally said, "If Mother wants to do it, then I won't object, as long as the boys are looked after."

"Lady Parker said the boys could attend school, too. Please say you'll take the jobs. I would be so happy knowing I would just have to walk across the garden to see my family."

Our talk was interrupted by Mr. Murphy's return to take me back to the castle. As I hugged my mother and father goodbye, my Da smiled and said, "Tell your good Lady that we will be very happy to accept both her offers and we can be ready to start in a fortnight."

Chapter 4

The two weeks passed very quickly and the cart sent to bring my family to Castle Chonamara arrived bearing my family and all their worldly goods. Father had managed to find a tenant to rent grandfather's cottage so he would have additional money to put away in what he called his "rainy day" fund. He never said, but I knew he was hoping to save enough money to help my brothers get a good start in life once they were grown.

Lady Parker and Miss Amelia were there to greet them and they took great delight in showing my mother around her new home, which had been cleaned and freshly painted before their arrival. As for Da, all he wanted to do was walk the gardens which would now be his domain. I don't think I've even seen my parents look more happy and content. Life was good.

Lady Parker seemed enchanted with my younger brothers and they adored her. When she noticed the only toys they had were sticks gathered from the woods with which they would sword fight, she took them up to castle's attic and gave them all the toys that had belonged to Master James, when he was their age. Their favorite was the big dapple-gray rocking horse. They took turns rocking on it every spare moment.

It wasn't long before they were begging to help out in the stables after school and on the weekends so they could be near real horses. Lady Parker was glad to give her permission and also pay them a small wage for their work, as long as Mother said their schoolwork was satisfactory and they listened carefully to old Mr. Murphy. After all, the stable was Mr. Murphy's domain just as the garden was now my father's.

Once Mother had the house in order, she began to make plans with Lady Parker for the reopening of the school. It was decided that classes would begin after the Christmas holidays. That would allow enough time for the new books Mother requested to arrive and the villagers to be informed of the school's reopening.

It was also about this time when Lady Parker decided she would reintroduce the tradition of the Christmas Eve Ball. The castle suddenly became a virtual beehive of activity.

The weeks leading up to the Ball brought many strangers to the castle. There were milliners to design and sew the new ball gowns for Lady Parker and Miss Amelia. There were musicians auditioning and entertainers of all sorts. There was also a visit from Lord Ashworth, an old family friend of Lady Parker's, and his son, Winston. Lord Ashworth was a handsome man not many years the senior of Lady Parker and a widower. He stayed for a fortnight and all the staff found him to be gentle and kind to everyone and especially attentive to Lady Parker. All of us who worked below stairs thought there was a romance in the making. We couldn't have been more wrong. You see, it later emerged that the object of the visit was to introduce Amelia to his son Winston. Lady Parker had known Winston from a young boy and thought he might make a good match for the shy Amelia.

Winston was a tall young man with fashionably long, sandy hair and gentle, deep set brown eyes. Like Amelia, he was also quiet and studious, but when engaged in conversation with her, he became quite animated. It was my duty, as her lady's maid, to chaperone the young couple as they walked the grounds of the castle and gardens beyond. Amelia took great pride in showing off the gardens she so loved and judging by the look on the young man's face, he too was charmed by the gardens, as well as by my mistress.

On this one particular day, a week into their visit, I had tarried behind the couple as they walked the paths to give them just enough privacy as possible while still remaining respectable. We hadn't ventured far when I heard Lady Parker call from the castle steps that tea was ready. Turning to wave an acknowledgment that I had heard her, I turned back to see a flushed faced Winston quickly drop Amelia's hand.

"Mistress Amelia, tea is ready," was all I said pretending I had not witnessed anything out of the ordinary.

Looking back over my shoulder, I smiled as I saw Winston offer his arm to Amelia as they followed me up the path into the castle. I had always known that Lady Parker was a very wise lady but after meeting the young man who she would have for her daughter, I knew she was much more than that.

That evening as I helped Mistress Amelia undress and prepare for bed she was unusually quiet. Brushing her hair, as she sat facing the vanity mirror, I ventured to say, "I like Master Winston. He seems so thoughtful and kind."

Glancing at her reflection in the mirror, I watched as her cheeks took on a rosy glow as she replied enthusiastically, "Oh Yes, Cathleen. He's so smart, too. There isn't anything he doesn't know and he loves the gardens just as much as I do."

I just smiled and nodded. Our Mistress Amelia was in love.

The rest of the visit saw the couple grow closer and when Master Winston and his father left they promised to return for the Christmas Eve Ball.

The days running up to the ball were extremely busy for everyone in the castle, especially the staff. Bedrooms that hadn't been used in years had to be opened and aired out for guests who would be staying overnight. Even Mr. Murphy was busy in the stables as he prepared sleighs to carry the guests on sleigh rides through the estate. My brothers were only too happy to help polish the beautiful sleighs since Mr. Murphy promised them a ride to our village when he went to pick up supplies. Cook was busy baking mince pies and all manner of Christmas cakes and puddings for the upcoming festivities.

The arrival of Lord Ashford and Winston only added to the excitement in the castle, as all the staff watched and waited to see if an announcement would be made at the ball. I accompanied Amelia and Winston on sleigh rides around the estate and I was touched by his gentle ways with her. I couldn't help but smile as I watched him gently tuck the lap blankets over Amelia's legs, fully aware that the young couple was undoubtedly holding hands under the cover of the blankets.

The ballroom was decorated with holly and ivy and one entire corner was taken up by the largest Christmas tree anyone in these mountains had ever seen. At Amelia's request, the tree was taken from outside the estate so as not to anger the Sidhe. Beautiful glass ornaments of all sizes and shapes hung from the branches of the lovely tree and twinkled brilliantly like the stars on a clear winter night when they caught the flicker of light from the hundreds of candles burning in the great hall. Wreaths made of all manner of greenery tied with beautiful tartan bows hung at the windows to commemorate the Parker and Ashford's ties to Scotland. The massive marble fireplace was adorned with holly and ivy and decorated with red ribbons and white flowers from her ladyship's greenhouse. As was the Irish tradition, a candle was lit in every window to welcome any strangers who may be passing in the night.

It came as no surprise to me when Lady Parker and Lord Ashford, joining hands, rose from their seats at the pre-ball dinner and jointly announced the engagement of their children. The ball was opened by Lady Parker and Lord

Ashford leading their guests in dance. They were quickly followed onto the dance floor by Amelia on the arm of her future husband as they enjoyed their first dance together. Watching from the wings, my heart swelled with joy and pride at seeing my shy, gentle lady looking confident and radiant as she twirled around the ballroom.

It was well past midnight when the ball finally ended and the guests who were staying over had climbed the stairs to their rooms and those leaving began to make their way to the front drive where their drivers waited patiently with the carriages. Arm in arm, Lady Parker and Lord Ashford and the newly engaged couple waved them off as they wished each and everyone one of them a Happy Christmas before retiring for the evening. Tomorrow would be a busy day for the staff, as they strived to make everything perfect for the newly engaged couple and Lady Parker and her guests.

Chapter 5

Christmas Day dawned bright but bitterly cold. All of us who worked below stairs had been up long before the day dawned to clean the massive fireplaces and lay the fires used to warm the high ceiling rooms of the castle. We had all finished our duties and set the long table in the formal dining room for breakfast for the family and their guests before we sat down to our own breakfast in the kitchen below. Despite all the work preparing for the family's celebrations of today, the staff was in a jovial mood. Tomorrow was Boxing Day and it meant a day of celebrations for the staff. Lady Parker had announced that on the day after Christmas all who worked at the castle and on the estate were to have a paid day off with the family taking care of their own needs and the needs of the animals that required feeding. Our benevolent Lady had instructed cook to prepare an abundance of food for the Christmas feast so the family could share what remained with the staff. It was to be a real day of rest for the staff and she didn't want anyone having to cook. We were all instructed to assemble in the ballroom after the family dinner on Christmas night and we were all pleasantly surprised to see the amount of gaily wrapped packages under the tree. There were presents carefully chosen for each staff member and baskets of food and sweets to share with our families. Miss Amelia presented me with a shawl of the finest Aran Merino wool to replace the one that had grown threadbare after years of wear. Lady Parker, knowing my love of reading, gifted me with a beautiful leather bound book of Irish folklore and legends.

It was wonderful to be standing in the beautifully decorated room with my family as we received our gifts. After everyone received their gifts, there was mulled cider for all assembled before we bid a joyous goodnight to the family and left to join our own families.

I stayed overnight with Ma and Da at their cottage in the gardens. It was so nice to see her being able to just sit and enjoy the feast our baskets contained and not having to cook for Da and my brothers. I had never seen my parents as content as since they moved here to the Castle. As for my brothers, they seemed to thrive in the new environment.

After dinner, Mother and I sat in the parlor in front of the fireplace drinking our tea and talking while Da and the boys played card games in the kitchen.

"So, what do you think of Miss Amelia's young man?" asked mother.

"He's lovely, Ma. He's ever so gentle and attentive to our Amelia. I have never met a couple more suited for each other. They both have the same interests and he respects her intelligence and that is a very rare thing these days, don't you agree?"

"I certainly do. I was very lucky in the same respect with your own father. He never resented my book learning but was proud of it and it worked well for us. I respected his special skills in the gardens and he respected mine in the classroom," said Ma as she looked lovingly at my father.

Getting up and going into the kitchen, Mother called back to me, "More tea, Cathleen?"

"Yes, please."

Coming back into the parlor, she poured the tea and asked, "So, when will the wedding be held?"

"They are talking about July."

"Oh my, that is soon. Everyone is going to be very busy at the castle. It takes a lot of planning for a society wedding," replied Ma.

Setting my cup down, my mind roamed back to the White Horse. I thought surely, the Sidhe would now be content with this family living on their land and happy with the changes brought

about by Lady Parker. And they must have
been. The young couple decided that the
wedding was to be held within the gardens
they both so loved and the Sidhe honored the
young couple by bringing forth the most
spectacular display of flowers even my father
said he had ever seen..

After the wedding, Miss Amelia and her new
husband left on a Grand Tour of Europe, gifted
to them by Winston's doting father, who had
grown to love Amelia as the daughter he never
had. Life was good and happiness reigned at
Castle Chonamara...at least for the moment.

Chapter 6

In the 1880's, the Irish Land Acts were enacted allowing many struggling farmers the ability to purchase the lands they worked. For others who could not afford to purchase their land, it made allowance for the lowering of rents by their landlords. While this virtually ended the era of the absentee landlords in Ireland, our estate remained unaffected by the new laws. This was all due to the benevolence of Lady Parker, who had implemented these changes on her own, five years before the laws were enacted.

It was the day before my twenty-seventh birthday in the year 1882 when she walked up the drive dressed in mourning black and dragging the young boy behind her. She walked right up the front steps and boldly knocked at the front door.

Answering the door, I asked, "May I help you?"

"Unless you are Lady Parker, then I doubt it very much. I am here to see Lady Parker," she sharply replied.

Opening the door, I led the way into the Morning Room and motioning to the settee said, "Please wait in here. I shall announce you. Whom may I say is calling?"

Pushing up her veil and removing her hat, she turned and faced me as she haughtily replied, "You may tell her, Mrs. James Parker and her son."

She was a tall woman and well-formed and until her face was revealed anyone would have thought her a handsome woman. Once the veil was lifted, it was impossible to draw the same conclusion. Her small beady eyes were deep set and void of any emotion. From the large mole on the side of her mouth grew a singular black hair. Her nose was long with a huge lump at its bridge and her thin lips were set in an unattractive sneer.

66

As I walked from the room and turned to close the door behind me I was stunned to witness the woman roughly push the young lad into the closest chair as she said, "Sit there and don't open your mouth or you'll get the back of my hand."

I found my Lady in the library standing and staring out the front window at the drive and the lake beyond. As I knocked and entered the room, she turned to me and quietly said, "I was looking out at the waters as our guests arrived so there is no need to tell me who they are. I would recognize the child anywhere. He could be James at that age brought back to life. Please show them in and order tea for us and cakes and hot cocoa for the child. It's a chilly day and he must be cold."

I could hear the warmth and concern in her voice when she mentioned the child and I struggled with whether or not I should mention what I had just witnessed in the morning room but merely nodded and did as I was told.

I so wished Lady Amelia and Lord Winston had not left a fortnight ago to visit his father's estates in Scotland. They would know what to do in these circumstances.

When I returned to the library with the tea, I found Lady Parker sitting white-faced and looking down at a document in her hand. As I placed the tea tray on the table between the two women, she raised her eyes to me and with a quiet voice said, "Cathleen will you have the maids make up the guest room for Lady Parker and Mr. James' room for my grandson?"

Backing out of the room, I went quickly to the kitchen and passed the message onto Mrs. Brown. The old housekeeper looked at me as though I had lost all my wits but ordered the maids to follow our Lady's instructions. After the maids were on their way up the back servants' stairs and out of ear shot, I slumped into the nearest chair and looked up at Mrs.

Brown as I said, "I have a feeling nothing good is going to come from this."

Sitting down opposite me, Mrs. Brown whispered, "Now tell me everything you know."

After telling her what had transpired, she nodded as she said, "I was wondering when one of Master James' bastards would come crawling out of the woodwork. With his low morals, I'm surprised there hasn't been more than just this one."

"Our Lady called the woman Lady Parker and she was looking at what looked like a legal document. It must be proof of their marriage."

The wise old housekeeper just nodded and rubbed her wrinkled chin thoughtfully as she said, "Papers can be as phony as some people. I know people who can check them out."

Before I could say another word she continued, "You best be checking on our good Lady and not a word to her of my plan, understand? No sense getting her hopes up if the child is legitimate."

"So what does this mean if he is Master James' legitimate son?" I asked.

Shaking her head she solemnly replied, "If he is then he would be the rightful heir to the castle and maybe even her ladyship's personal fortune."

Trying to compose myself, I slowly climbed the stairs and knocked softly at the library door. When I was told to enter, I found our Lady sitting alone on the settee with the young boy. The child's mother was nowhere to be seen.

Looking up and smiling, Lady Parker said to the child, "Jamie, I would like you to meet Cathleen. Cathleen has been here at the castle since she was your age and she knows all the good places to play."

Before I could even greet the young boy, he rose to his feet and bowed to me saying softly, "It is a pleasure to meet you, Miss Cathleen. I hope you will show me around when you have time. I love playing hide and seek."

Dropping to a curtsy, I couldn't help but smile and replied warmly, "I will be happy to show you all the good places to hide Master Jamie."

Gently running her fingers through the child's hair, Lady Parker looked up and said, "Jamie's mother was exhausted from their journey and has retired to her room. Would you be kind enough to show my grandson to his room and give him a tour of the castle on your way?"

Nodding and stretching my hand out to the child I replied, "Yes, ma'am. I'd be happy to. Come along Master Jamie.

I spent the best part of an hour showing the shy young boy around the inside of the castle and was impressed by his polite and gentle manner. Despite the impression of haughtiness I had felt during my brief encounter with his mother, it was obvious she had raised the child to have manners. Her behavior towards him I had witnessed in the morning room still plagued me. After showing Master Jamie to his room and helping him unpack his bag I told him I would return when it was time for dinner.

Before I left he looked up at me with his sad, lash-fringed eyes, so like his father's, and whispered, "was this really my father's room?'

"Yes, Master Jamie, it was."

Looking around the room, as if trying to find something familiar, his eyes finally alighted on the portrait of Master James as a young boy with Lady Parker, which hung over the fireplace and asked, "Is that my father with my grandmother?"

"Yes, Master Jamie."

"I never met him, you know."

"No, Master Jamie, I didn't know."

Suddenly becoming very quiet he bowed and thanked me for my kindness before I left him alone to rest before dinner.

As I walked down the main staircase, I found Lady Parker waiting at the foot of the stairs.

"Is the child settling in alright, Cathleen?" she asked.

"Yes ma'am. He's in his room resting."

"Has his mother checked on him?" she asked.

"No ma'am. He's alone."

"How very strange," she replied raising her eyebrows as she turned and went back into the library closing the door behind her.

I did not see our Lady until the evening meal was served. When I entered the dining room with young Jamie, the tension in the air could have been cut with a knife. She sat rigid and deathly white in her chair. As we entered, the child's mother abruptly pushed back her chair and loudly announced, "I know my rights. My son is the legitimate heir now and all of this will be his once he reaches his majority but until then I will manage everything for him and right now I wish to walk in my gardens."

I could see the young boy at my side stiffen at the sound of his mother's voice as left the room slamming the door behind her.

Looking across at her grandson, Lady Parker gently asked, "Are you hungry Jamie? I didn't know what you liked, so I had Cook make an assortment of things. I hope something here will appeal to you."

Shyly looking across at the older woman, young Master Jamie suddenly smiled brightly and replied, "Everything looks wonderful ma'am."

"You may call me Grandmother or Grandmamma, whichever pleases you my child, for you are my only son's child and we are all very glad you have found your way to us."

The child had barely begun eating when my father barged into the room unannounced and shouted, "Come quickly, Lady Parker. There's been an accident in the garden."

"What has happened Mr. Cullen? Is anyone injured?"

Glancing quickly from the child to Lady Parker he said, "The wall we were erecting has collapsed onto a bench where the child's mother was sitting. The workmen are removing the fallen stones now and Dr. Burke has been sent for."

By the time we reached the wall, Jamie's mother was lying covered with a blanket and was being tended by my mother. When I saw the blood oozing from the injured woman's mouth and saw the look on my mother's face, I realized that the outcome was grim. Although still conscious, Jamie's mother never once uttered a word of comfort to her son, who was clinging tightly to Lady Parker's hand, but muttered repeatedly about a huge white horse pushing the wall down on her. Most of those gathered around assumed the dying woman was hallucinating, but Lady Parker and I both knew that the beast had been sent by the fairies to protect their sacred grounds from this woman. Despite who owned the castle, the gardens belonged to no human they belonged to the Sidhe.

By the time Dr. Burke arrived at the scene there was little doubt to any of us the outcome of this tragedy. Within minutes of his initial exam, his fingers sought a vein in her throat before looking anxiously at Lady Parker and shaking his head. The newly arrived widow of Master James had gone to meet her maker.

Quickly stooping down and wrapping her arms around young Master Jamie, Lady Parker said ever so gently, "Let's go back to the house, shall we? The good doctor will stay here and take care of your mother."

The poor child never said a word. He just looked around at all those gathered there with his eyes wide with shock. Taking hold of Lady Parker's hand, he slowly followed her from the garden to the castle. I stayed behind for a few moments to speak with my mother and father before quickly returning to the castle. By the time I arrived back at the castle, Mrs. Brown had brought a tea tray to the library where Lady Parker was attempting to console her grandson.

As I entered the room, Lady Parker had pulled her grandson's chair close to hers and was listening intently to what he was whispering to her. As I moved closer I heard Master Jamie say, "She wasn't my mother."

Lady Parker looked startled and began to say something when Jamie interrupted her and continued, "She was the wardrobe mistress at the theater where my real mother worked until she became sick and died last year. Her name was Gertrude Blum and she and my mother were friends of a sort. At least my mother confided in her that my father was James Parker and that he had a big estate here in these mountains. My father used to come to the theater a lot when he was in London on business."

I think I was less shocked than Lady Parker because I had seen how the child was ill treated by the woman who claimed to be his mother. Poor Lady Parker was dumbstruck and sat very still waiting for the child to continue.

"I never met my father. I think he stopped coming to see my mother before I was born," continued the child as he arose from his chair and began pacing back and forth and tearfully asked, "What shall become of me now?"

Gently taking his hands in hers, Lady Parker continued, "Despite who your mother was, you are the legitimate son of my son and as such you are the heir to this castle and all its lands."

Suddenly bowing his head, with heaving shoulders, he asked, "But am I?"

"Are you what, child?"

"Am I legitimate?"

"Your mother, I mean Ms. Blum showed me a document that seems to attest to your legitimacy," replied Lady Parker.

Shaking his head, the young boy replied through tears, "Things, like people, are not always what they seem."

Regaining her composure and rising to her feet, Lady Parker again took the child in her arms and said, "I will have my solicitor check the document if it will ease your troubled mind, but no matter what the outcome, you are still my grandson and I love you and I will take care of you from this day onward. So no more tears."

Turning to me, Lady Parker asked, "Cathleen, will you take Jamie down to the kitchen and get him some sweet tea and something to eat while I go speak with your father? Please apologize to Mrs. Brown for me. I'm afraid I've let the tea she brought us grow cold."

"Certainly, ma'am, you go ahead and I'll take this tray back to the kitchen. Master Jamie and I can go check on the new foal at the stables when he is done his tea, if he'd like."

The mention of the new foal finally brought a smile to the young boy's face and as Lady Parker swept past us leaving the library she placed a hand on my shoulder and said, "You're a good girl, Cathleen. You are wise beyond your years. I don't know what I would do without you."

As time went on Master Jamie settled into life here at Castle Chonamara and neither Lady Parker nor I ever mentioned the White Horse's involvement in Ms. Blum's death. The summer was spent with the nature loving child exploring the gardens with his grandmother and Miss Amelia, who had returned from her travels with

Lord Winston in Scotland. The Sidhe seemed to accept the arrival of the young boy as he carefully played in their garden. So it didn't surprise me when I found him and Lady Amelia sitting in front of the wisteria carrying on an animated conversation with the Sidhe.

He quickly became friends with my brothers and was often seen at the stables and soon became an excellent horseman. It was early in autumn that the news came from Lady Parker's solicitor in London that the document which would have made Master Jamie the heir to Castle Chonamara was indeed a forgery and he was indeed illegitimate. This news had little effect on the way Lady Parker or the rest of the family or staff treated the young boy, for he had become a beloved member of the family. Young Jamie joined with my brothers and the other local children at the estate school and soon, at the recommendation of my mother, Lady Parker arranged for his education to continue at Eton near Windsor, England the following autumn. To my mother's delight she had also commissioned a place at Eton for my oldest brother so he would have more opportunities in life and so the boys could remain close and not feel lonely while away at school.

Chapter 7

I was approaching my thirty-fourth birthday in 1889. There had been no sign of a visitation by the White Horse and it was nearing seven years since his last appearance.

The Sidhe seemed to have disappeared from the garden since the elder Lord Ashford died and Amelia and her husband, now the new Lord Ashford, left the castle to handle his vast estates in Scotland. Our dear Lady Parker became very melancholy, missing her daughter and the granddaughter the couple had presented her with just a year after their return from their honeymoon, and Master Jamie who was away at school.

Since Winston's return to his own family estates, it had been necessary for Lady Parker to hire an estate manager to handle the daily affairs of running such a large estate. There were three very capable men interviewing for the position and two of them had excellent references but Lady Parker finally decided on

Angus MacCallan. It wasn't that his references were any better than the other men and the truth be told, they were not. He had been released from two of his former positions for failing to obey the owner's instructions. When I saw this on his letters of reference, I begged Lady Parker to enquire further into what these instructions had entailed. Surely, they must have been of an important nature if they were grounds for immediate dismissal.

The day of his interview, I personally escorted him into the library. He was a tall, well-formed man of late middle age with graying hair and the darkly tanned skin found on men who spent their days working outdoors. Although I instinctively felt uncomfortable in his presence, Lady Parker seemed to instantly warm to the big Scotsman. Perhaps he reminded our Lady of happier times in her youth when she lived in Scotland and her children were small, before the troubles brought about by Master James had forced them to move to Ireland. Or perhaps she was flattered by the attention he lavished upon her. By the time they had finished their tea, the references had been forgotten and he had secured the position of Estate Manager of Castle Chonamara.

As I escorted him from the library to the front door, I was shocked to feel an unwelcomed pat on my behind. As I turned to confront him, the devil just winked at me and tipped his hat, whistling as he strode brazenly down the front steps.

His superior attitude began on that first day and continued growing more and more outlandish with every day that passed. There were numerous complaints from the maids concerning unwelcome advances and inappropriate remarks. Unlike the rest of the staff, he refused to enter the castle through the service entrance and brazenly used the front entrance reserved for the family and their guests.

Although he was given the cottage reserved for the estate manager and had access to meals with the staff, he began to spend more and more time in the evenings at the castle and within months he was dining with Lady Parker every evening.

It wasn't until the staff began making remarks did I venture to broach the subject with Lady Parker. The perfect moment arose the next day while delivering her breakfast tray. Lady Parker was sitting up in her bed looking younger and happier than I had seen her since Amelia and Jamie left.

"Good Morning, Lady Parker. You are looking rested this morning," I said as I placed the tray on her night table and pulled back the drapes letting the morning sun shine into the bedchamber.

"Good Morning, Cathleen. Looks like a beautiful, bright day."

"It is indeed. It would be a nice day for a walk in the garden."

"I think you're right, Cathleen. I haven't spent much time in the garden since our dear Amelia left. Would you accompany me?"

"Of course, Lady Parker, I'd like that very much," I replied as I collected her breakfast tray and headed for the door.

"Shall we meet in the front hall in an hour?"

"That will work out perfectly," I replied.

As I made my way down the staircase towards the kitchen below stairs, I began to mull over in my mind exactly how I would broach the subject of the estate manager's behavior.

An hour later, as I was waiting in the center hall for Lady Parker, Angus MacCallan abruptly entered through the front door, as if he owned the place. Even his deeply tanned skin couldn't hide the flush of anger showing on his face as he bellowed, "I need to see Lady Parker now!"

Before I could admonish him, I heard Lady Parker's footsteps coming down the staircase.

"Whatever is the problem, Angus?"

Still shouting, the blustering Scotsman replied, "He may be your head gardener but I am the estate manager and he takes orders from me. I will not tolerate his insubordination!"

Seeing the flush on my face at the mention of my father in such a manner, Lady Parker grabbed MacCallan by his arm and unceremoniously steered him into the library shutting the door firmly behind them.

As I stood open-mouthed at what had just occurred, the library door opened again and Lady Parker said softly, "I won't be long Cathleen. Please go ahead and I'll meet you shortly in the garden, as we planned."

Just nodding my agreement, I started for the door as the library door closed again, but not before I heard the Scotsman sweeten his tone of voice as he tried to convince our Lady of his innocence in whatever had occurred in the gardens this morning.

As I entered the walled garden, I looked about hoping to find my father to ask him what had transpired, but he was nowhere to be found. As I sat on the marble bench waiting for Lady Parker, I heard the sound of whispered voices. Pushing the leaves of the bushes aside, I found a group of no less than ten Sidhe. Gasping out loud, the Sidhe stopped their chattering and turned to stare directly at me. Suddenly, the larger of the Sidhe stepped forward and stared at me with the most incredible blue eyes I had ever seen. Squinting from the sunlight, caused by my movement of the branches, the Sidhe said, "I recognize you. You're Miss Amelia's friend."

Unable to speak, I just nodded my assent.

"I've been chosen to warn you. We don't like that man who wears a dress like a woman. He has been disturbing things in our garden. He brings those animals of his into our garden and they dig up our flowers and foul it. This is not a toilet for his beasts. This is our home and we will not be sniffed at or chased about by the creatures. That nice gardener chased them out this morning and saved poor Aurora from being killed and then that bad man came and argued with him and laid his hands on him. You need to tell Lady Parker that we will not tolerate this. She must put a stop to it or we will. Do you understand my meaning?"

Still frozen to the spot and unable to speak, all I could do was nod my response. I was still sitting there dumbfounded when I heard the garden door open and saw Lady Parker coming slowly up the path.

Dropping down on the bench beside me she sighed loudly before saying, "So much ado about nothing."

Finally able to regain my voice I said, "Nothing? Lady Parker you must stop Mr.

MacCallan from letting his dogs have the run of the walled gardens."

"Really Cathleen, what possible harm can two wee dogs cause?"

I hesitated a moment before I finally decided to tell her what I had witnessed in the garden this morning. "Lady Parker, I do not wish to tempt fate or bring up past events that are painful to you, but I have received a warning from the masters of the White Horse they wish me to convey to you."

Suddenly becoming very quiet and slightly raising her eyebrow she replied, "Are you sure what you're about to tell me is true and not something you've fabricated to protect your father from being disciplined?"

Shocked by her cold, accusing attitude towards me, I abruptly rose to me feet and exclaimed, "Lady Parker, I have never told you anything but the truth and it deeply pains me you would believe otherwise. You may choose to believe me, or not, and you may disciple my father as you wish, but I must give you the Sidhe's message."

"Sidhe? And who is this Sidhe?" she asked.

"They are not a 'who'; they are a 'they.' They are the fairies that call these lands their own. These gardens and the very estate in which we stand are sacred ground to them."

"Really Cathleen, do you really expect me to believe this?"

Looking at her strangely, I replied, "Lady Parker, you have seen with your own eyes what the White Horse is capable of. He is going to come again if Mr. MacCallan does not keep his dogs out of their garden."

She hesitated for a moment before her expression changed and then rising to her feet and taking my hands she said, "I will speak to Angus about the dogs."

With that she turned and swept from the garden without another word. Instinctively I knew that things had changed between my good lady and I, and it wasn't for the better.

After she left, I went in search of my father. As I walked up to the front door of the cottage my parents shared, I overheard my mother's raised voice, "How dare he put his hands on you. I will speak to Lady Parker immediately."

In a calmer voice, I heard my father reply, "It's nothing my dear. I will handle this myself. I have a meeting with Lady Parker tomorrow anyway and I'll discuss today's events with her then."

Waiting just a few moments, I knocked softly on the door and called, "It's Cathleen."

Swinging the door open, my Da wrapped me in his arms in a warm hug as he asked, "What brings you here on this fine morning?"

I was shocked to see the large bandage on the side of my father's head and reaching my hand up to touch it asked, "My goodness Da, what happened?"

Shrugging it off, he turned his back and walked back to sit in his chair by the fire and returned to his tea saying, "It's nothing, just a little accident in the garden. It's nothing to worry yourself over."

Mother, who couldn't abide anything but the telling of the truth, turned her back also and went into the kitchen on the pretense of fixing me a cup of tea. As soon as she was out of my father's line of vision she motioned for me to follow. Taking her hint, I continued making polite conversation with Da until she called from the kitchen, "Do you have time for a cuppa, Cathleen?"

Excusing myself, I called back, "Just a quick one, Mother."

As soon as we were seated closely around the table she whispered, "It was that Scottish devil. Your father complained about the mess his hounds were making in the garden and asked if he wouldn't let them get their exercise somewhere else. He then told your father that although he might be the head gardener that he had Lady Parker's ear, and if your Da didn't do what he said, he'd see Da was replaced and we were all out on our ears."

Taking a sip of the now lukewarm tea I said, "I don't believe Lady Parker would do anything like that Ma."

"I don't know Cathleen. He's been flaunting his dining with our Lady and has hinted to more than one of the staff that he is more than just an employee to her. It's not true, is it Cathleen?"

Carefully measuring my words I replied, "It is true that he does dine with her but I am sure that is the extent of it. Anything else is just wishful thinking on his part. You know Lady Parker has been very lonely since Miss Amelia and her family moved back to Scotland and Master Jamie has been away. I think he reminds her of happier days in Scotland, and he can be charming when it benefits him. Unfortunately, Lady Parker hasn't seen the other side of him, at least not yet. But she is a very wise woman and I don't think he can fool her for much longer."

Mother's tight grip on her cup relaxed at my assessment of the situation. Wiping her eyes with the corner of her apron she said, "I'm so glad you stopped by. I have been fretting all morning that we'd have to move from this home where we've been so happy."

Reaching across the table and covering her thin hand in mine I said, "I don't think there is any chance of that Ma. I am sure after Da speaks with Lady Parker tomorrow that Mr. MacCallan will not bother Da again. Now, I better be getting back to the castle but I'll stop in after dinner tomorrow night. If you need me for anything at all just send one of the boys for me."

Hugging my parents goodbye, I quickly made my way back through the gardens to the castle and my work.

The rest of the evening was quieter than recent weeks with Mr. MacCallan visibly missing from our lady's dinner table. Whispered gossip flowed through the downstairs as staff after staff repeated bits and pieces of conversations they had overheard between Lady Parker and himself. As for Lady Parker, she seemed quite herself as if nothing out of the ordinary had transpired.

The next morning again dawned bright and warm for this time of year and when I delivered Lady Parker's breakfast tray she asked, "Do you think we can finally have that walk in the garden that was interrupted yesterday? I feel the need for some fresh air."

"I would like that too. It's always lovely to walk in the gardens this time of year. I'll need to finish a few chores first. What time shall I meet you in the hall?"

"Well, I have a meeting with your father at 11:00, so how about in an hour?"

"That's fine. If there's nothing else you need, I'll get on with my chores."

Smiling with relief at seeing Lady Parker in such a good mood before her meeting with my Da eased my worried mind as I went on about my work.

As fate, or the Sidhe, would have it there was no need to worry about that morning's meeting.

Lady Parker looked lovely with the palest of lavender shawls wrapped around her narrow shoulders as she seemed to float down the stairs. Her mood was as light as her step, and I was anxious for our walk and hoped she might share with me the reason for her suddenly improved disposition.

We had just reached the drive surrounding the lake when she pulled an envelope from the pocket of her shawl, and giggling like a young girl said, "I have received a letter."

"I can see that my lady," I laughed out loud as she began to unfold it and read it aloud.

"Dear Grandmamma.

I hope this finds you well. I am writing to tell you that I hope to be with you in a fortnight. I have some time off from classes to study for my exams. I will be traveling first to Scotland and with any luck I can convince Amelia to join me on my journey home so we can all be together, if just for a short time.

Your loving grandson,

Jamie"

Clapping my hands together, I had to restrain myself from hugging Lady Parker at this wonderful news. It would be so good to see Miss Amelia and my friend Master Jamie.

Slipping her arm through mine, we left the drive and started down the lakeside path towards the gardens beyond. It was then we saw him as he seemed to fly over the top of the eight foot garden wall and glide across the still waters of the lake before disappearing under its waters.

I had just managed to grab Lady Parker's arm to try to prevent her from entering the garden when the gate swung open and Mr. MacCallan's two hounds came racing out as if the devil himself was chasing them. Alerted by the baying of the hounds, my father and the under-gardeners raced towards us, but not before Lady Parker pushed the gate open wide, screamed once, and fainted dead away.

As I knelt by her side, cradling her head in my lap, my father stood staring and open-mouthed at the sight he beheld. Speaking in a hushed voice he placed his hand on my head and pushing it downward sternly said, "Look away Cathleen. This is the stuff of nightmares."

My father was right, but it was too late to save me from the nightmares that would be the cause of many sleepless nights, for I had never seen a body so badly mutilated as that of Angus MacCallan. The Sidhe had taken their revenge and once again the White Horse had been their emissary of death.

Chapter 8

I turned thirty-seven in 1892. It had been a terrible year for me. First, my mother died suddenly of what was believed to be heart failure and within just six months my Da followed her with a stroke. My brothers came home for the funerals, but they had their own families now so once again I was left alone at the castle with an aging Lady Parker.

After the gruesome death of Angus MacCallan, Lady Parker's health began to slowly deteriorate. The only things that kept her going these past years were the visits from Miss Amelia and her young daughter, Anne, and Jamie.

It was spring when Miss Amelia came for her annual visit. After having tea with her mother, she took me aside and whispered, "Can we walk in the garden? I am worried about Mother."

Nodding my agreement, I smiled and replied, "I'll meet you at the bench in five minutes."

I was a bit surprised to find Amelia leaning forward and talking and laughing with what I could only assume were her Sidhe friends. They had been noticeably quiet these last few years, not even appearing for any of Miss Amelia's previous visits. As she continued her animated conversation, I sat patiently on the garden bench waiting and fuming.

When she had finished, she turned to me and taking my hands in hers said, "The Sidhe asked me to tell you that they are very sorry you had to see what happened to that evil man and they hope it didn't cause you much distress."

Thinking of how badly Lady Parker's health had been affected, I started to bristle and replied, "They should be ashamed of themselves. They could have waited one more day and let your mother handle Angus

MacCallan. What she saw greatly affected her health, not to mention the horrible nightmares I've had these many years."

Amelia said nothing but continued to hold my hand and wait patiently as I vented my anger at the Sidhe and the White Horse.

Finally placing her hand on my shoulder, she said, "They sensed how upset everyone was with them and that is why they didn't come out to speak with me on my last visits. But now they felt we should know. There were things the Sidhe knew that we did not and they had to act when they did to try to protect my mother." Completely confused I waited for Amelia to continue. "Did you never wonder why Mr. MacCallan suddenly decided to change his habits and began to walk his hounds in the walled garden and not in the woods as before?"

"Not really. I thought he was doing it to spite my father," I replied.

"The Sidhe caught him that morning collecting leaves from the cherry laurel and knew then he must have had been mixing it in my mother's wine when he began dining with her. He was slowly poisoning her."

"Poisoning her?" I exclaimed as my hand went to my mouth.

"Yes, the foliage of the cherry laurel is naturally rich in the poison cyanide. They had already noticed a change in my mother's appearance, a slight bluish tint to her skin, so when they caught him collecting the leaves they knew they must act immediately. So you see they were not being completely selfish. Not this time, at least," explained Amelia.

"But why would he want to poison your mother? That doesn't make sense," I replied.

"I don't think he intended to cause her death. I think he was trying to weaken her to the point he could make himself indispensable to her and perhaps even gain access to her money."

Knowing the vindictiveness the Sidhe were capable of, I was slow to accept this revelation by the fairies. Unfortunately, their explanation for their action was confirmed by Doctor Turner, a specialist brought in from London to evaluate and treat Lady Parker. His tests confirmed that Lady Parker had indeed been receiving small doses of Cyanide which slowly deprived her nervous system of the oxygen that was essential to life. Once the diagnosis was received, Doctor Turner began to aggressively treat her condition, but the damage that had been done could not be reversed. It became apparent that Lady Parker was in need of constant care. Once the sad prognosis was revealed, Miss Amelia announced that she would be taking her mother home to Scotland with her.

I was to remain behind and keep the castle running and the staff employed with the help of someone I had yet to meet. Lord Winston was eager to ensure his mother-in-law's estate be properly managed and sent me a letter of introduction for a Mr. Ian O'Brien, informing me that I was to expect his arrival.

Despite the letter of introduction and the glowing references, nothing could have prepared me for the arrival of Ian O'Brien.

It was early one blustery, rainy Sunday morning as I was on my hands and knees cleaning out the library fireplace when the front door bell signaled the arrival of the stranger. Covered with soot, I wiped my hands on my apron, pushed back the hair that had escaped my bun and hurried to the door. I could barely get the door open when he blew in like a whirling dervish. His large brimmed hat, dripping with rain, covered his face, but I could just make out his startling green eyes. Not a word was said as he took off his rain soaked coat and pulled his hat off and dropped them onto my outstretched arm.

Finally regaining my voice, I asked, "May I help you, sir?"

Staring intently at my face, he replied, "I believe I am expected. I'm Ian O'Brien. Is Mrs. Cullen available?"

Before I could answer, he boldly reached out and stroked my cheek with his fingertips. Startled and stepping back at his familiarity, he quickly said, "I beg your pardon, but you had soot very close to your eye. I'm sorry if I have offended you. If you will call Mrs. Cullen, I won't trouble you anymore."

Quickly regaining my composure, I replied, "I am Miss Cullen. Welcome to Castle Chonamara, Mr. O'Brien. Pardon my appearance; I have been cleaning the fireplace, as you may well have guessed."

He smiled now as he said, "Shouldn't that be the job of one of the housemaids, Miss Cullen?"

"It would be, but today being Sunday, I have given the maids the morning off to attend church and see their families. They will be back after lunch, but in the meantime I do what I can."

"You can't possible clean and start all the fires here," He commented as his eyes cast around the hallway.

"With no family in residence at this time, we only keep the fires lit in the library and the kitchen below stairs," I replied.

Suddenly remembering my manners, I said, "You must be cold and hungry from your trip. If you would like to wait in the library, I'll see about tea."

Nodding his agreement, I opened the door to the library and quickly lit the fire before leaving him alone and headed downstairs to the kitchen.

Heading first to the washroom, I quickly washed my face and hands then re-pinned my hair before slipping on a clean apron.

When I returned to the library a little while later, he was bent over stoking the fire. I couldn't help but notice that as well as having a handsome face, he was also well-formed. It was immediately obvious that this was a man who worked with his hands and not one who earned his living sitting behind a desk. I couldn't help but compare him to my beloved father.

As I entered the room, he quickly rose to his feet and immediately came to my side, lifting the heavily laden tray from my hands. Sitting it down on the table between the two chairs that faced the massive fireplace, he stood respectfully waiting for me to sit first, as if I was the lady of the house. Once seated, he reached for the teapot and poured my tea first before filling his own cup. I think it may have been then that I fell in love with Ian O'Brien.

Mr. O' Brien was a very capable manager of the estate. The front portico was the first thing he attacked and after carefully reviewing the original plans, he managed to rebuild it, wiping out all memories of the horror that had occurred there. He spent his days in the outside directing the progress of the gardeners and the men who maintained the castle and outbuildings. His evenings, after dinner, were spent handling the financial paperwork necessary for keeping the estate running and profitable. He had only been here a little over six months when he came clamoring down the stone steps to the kitchen one afternoon, yelling as he came, "Miss Cullen, are you down here?"

"Yes, Mr. O'Brien. I am just seeing to the dinner menu for this evening."

Standing with his hands clasped behind his back like a schoolboy being corrected for bad behavior, he stammered, "Yes, about dinner.

There will be two for dinner tonight in the dining room."

Having not been previously told to expect a guest, I asked, "Two, Mr. O'Brien?"

"Yes, Miss Cullen. If it's not too great an imposition, I would be grateful if you could dine with me tonight."

Feeling my face beginning to burn as the blush spread across my cheeks, I stuttered as I asked, "Me?"

A slight smile played across his full lips as he noticed my blush and replied, "Yes, Miss Cullen. I have some ideas to increase the amount of revenue coming into the estate and I would like your opinion as the castle's oldest employee."

With that he turned and clamored back up the steps again leaving me to fume over his 'oldest employee' remark and wonder exactly what he was planning and what it had to do with me. It didn't take long for me to find out.

Chapter 9

I took special care dressing for dinner that evening, his 'oldest employee' remark had really hurt my pride and I wanted to look my best. When I entered the dining room, I was surprised to find Mr. O'Brien pacing nervously in front of the fireplace.

As soon as I entered the room, he rushed to the table and pulled out my chair, then sat directly opposite me. My eyes immediately scanned the table laden with plates of meat and bowels of vegetables artfully arranged. There were even candles and flowers adorning the table. I knew in an instant that this certainly wasn't Cook's normal table setting.

Confused, I finally raised my eyes and found Mr. O'Brien staring at me with a silly grin on his face as he asked, "Will it do?"

Unable to think straight, all I could manage to say was, "Everything looks lovely, Mr. O'Brien."

Staring at me intently he said, "I thought we had agreed when I first arrived that you could call me Ian."

"I don't think that would be proper, Mr. O'Brien," I primly replied.

Placing some meat on my plate and then placing the bowls of vegetables within my reach, he didn't utter a word as he continued to fill his own plate. Just the sound of the silverware as it touched the plates could be heard as silence fell over the dining room.

"Miss Cullen, If you think that calling me by my Christian name wouldn't be proper then I dread to think how you'll feel about what I'm about to say," he said between mouthfuls.

"And what is that, Mr. O'Brien?" I asked, gaining Dutch courage from drinking the wine.

"I'm a simple man, Miss Cullen, so I will just say it right out. I have been in love with you ever since that first day when I wiped the soot from your lovely face and I would be honored if you would agree be my wife."

Unfortunately, for my dignity and Mr. O'Brien's freshly cleaned white shirt, I had just taken a large sip of claret which I promptly choked on and sprayed all over the front of him.

What he did next convinced me that my reply to his proposal was going to be yes. Instead of getting angry, as many men would under the circumstances, he immediately jumped to his feet and ran to my side asking, "Are you alright Cathleen? I'm so sorry, I didn't mean to startle you and make you choke. I'm such an idiot. What must you think of me?"

Recovered from my choking, I rose from my chair and I looked up into his concerned eyes and said, "What must I think of you? Well, Mr. O'Brien, I think you are the most caring, gentle man I have ever met and I, sir, will feel honored to be your wife."

The wedding was held in the village of my birth exactly one year to the day that Mr. O'Brien, or Ian, as I now called him, had blown into the castle that stormy morning and into my life. It was a quiet affair, with only my brothers and their families, Ian's old-maid school teacher sister and of course our friends at the castle attending. Cook had prepared a special wedding dinner for everyone attending and for .this special occasion we all dined together in the dining room, normally reserved for the family, followed by dancing in the ballroom. It was such a grand night and one I would cherish for all my years.

The next day, Ian moved my life's possessions into his house just opposite the one in which my parents had been so happy. I prayed, as I crossed the threshold of my new home, that I would be as happy here as my parents had been in their home. And for the four years I was.

Chapter 10

Ian continued to work very hard getting the estate back to its former glory. He had received a message from Sir Winston that a wealthy merchant was interested in letting the castle for a retreat for his wife who found the sounds of industrial Belfast too hard on her delicate nerves. They were to arrive in six months.

Hard as he might try, Ian was unable to find a gardener to replace our gardener, who had moved back to Dublin to be close to his family. In the end, more out of frustration than anything else, he took on a traveler who had shown up at the castle one morning asking for work. Rory Kelly had no references but Ian, bone-weary of trying to do his normal work and then maintain the garden, gave the man a chance.

In the beginning, Mr. Kelly worked out well. His work couldn't be compared to the work done by my father but he seemed to honestly do his best.

It was one evening after dinner while Ian was busy with the estate's paperwork; I decided to take a walk in the walled garden. I walked the familiar moss covered path heading for the bench where I had often sat with Lady Parker. As I walked, the bushes along the path began to move slightly as though something was following me step-by-step. Reaching my destination, I settled myself on the bench and waited. I knew they were watching me.

I sat there quietly just taking in the scents and sounds of the garden until the sky began to lose its light. As I started to rise to leave, I said, "If you have something to say to me, then I suggest you say it now. The sun is setting and it's getting cold and I have come away without my shawl."

As I started to walk away, the leader of the Sidhe made her presence known as she hopped from the bushes and settled herself on the bench and began talking quietly.

"I know you think we are evil but we only react to our home being threatened," she said as she stood and began pacing about her perch on the bench.

Looking down at her, I replied, "I admit that I have seen cause for some of your actions but there are other ways to protect your homes than by summoning the White Horse."

Shaking her head, she replied contritely "We have tried on many occasions to give you warnings so you could intervene."

In my heart, I had to admit that the Sidhe spoke the truth. There had been warnings but in most of those cases I had been unable to stop the offenses that had upset the fairies.

"So, why contact me now? I cautiously asked.

"That new man, who works in our garden...he is a thief," she pronounced.

I had always felt uneasy where Mr. Kelly was concerned but I never suspected him of thievery.

"What do you mean?" I asked.

"We saw him. He came into the garden one night after dark and he buried something by the bushes over in the corner of the garden. He had it in a burlap bag."

Knowing that the barn cat had lost the runt of her newest litter, I asked, "Didn't it occur to you that he could have been burying the remains of a small animal?"

Nodding her head up and down excitedly she replied, "Yes, we thought at first that was what he was doing, but then Flora said he kissed the bag and laughed out loud before covering it with dirt. Now why would he do that if there was a dead creature in the bag, Miss Cathleen?"

"He wouldn't. Thank you for telling me. I'll fetch my husband right away and we'll get to the bottom of this tonight," I replied as I swept out of the garden and ran the remaining distance to our cottage.

Ian was still at his desk working on the estate accounts when I pushed the door open and yelled, "Come with me Ian and bring a shovel."

Looking weary, a confused look crossed my dear husband's face, but without asking one question, he threw his jacket on and handed me my shawl before going outside and grabbing the shovel I kept leaning against the side of the cottage.

He followed me as I led the way into the walled garden and pointing to the corner of the garden I said, "Dig there."

Giving me a curious look, he began to dig until we heard the sound of metal touching metal. Reaching into the hole, Ian pulled out the burlap bag and emptied its contents on the ground.

"What the hell? How did you know this silver was buried here?"

"The Sidhe told me. They saw Rory Kelly bury it. What are you going to do, Ian?"

"We can't do anything right now. We're going to cover this back up for the time being. I can't accuse him right now because he'll deny burying this here and the only witness we have are the fairies. We'll have to catch him in the act."

The next evening I returned to the garden in hopes of talking again with the Sidhe. After just a few minutes, they appeared and shaking their heads to show their disapproval said, "We see the thief is still here."

"Yes, we have to catch him actually stealing something to have him arrested," I explained.

"Those things he takes belong to our friend Amelia and we won't have him stealing from her," they replied indignantly before vanishing.

I knew now that if Ian and I couldn't stop the looting of the castle, and soon, that there would be another visitation by their agent of death.

It was just two nights later when we noticed a strange light in the upstairs of the castle. Ian was out the door and making his way into the castle before I had even gotten my shawl on. As I raced past the lake, the wind began to pick up and usually calm waters of the lake began to churn. I knew he was coming.

I had just opened the front door and entered the hall when I saw the figures of two men wrestling in the upstairs hall. I gasped as I saw one man strike the other man causing him to lose his balance and fall all the way down the long staircase. Switching on the light, I ran toward the fallen figure and turning him over gazed into the green eyes of my husband. His neck had been broken in the fall and as I pulled him close to my chest, Kelly pushed past me and headed for the door and escape.

As I cradled my darling husband's head I yelled, 'You might have escaped from my husband Kelly but you won't escape what is waiting for you outside."

Hesitating for just a moment, he replied, "You must be mad with grief woman. I have already escaped."

I stayed with my husband, holding him in my arms until his body grew cold, knowing there was no need to rouse the staff to go after Kelly. I knew he wouldn't be allowed to get far.

Waiting at the bottom of the steps, Kelly found the vehicle for his escape. The White Horse stood docile and waiting for a rider. Grabbing the horse's mane, he pulled himself onto his back and giving him a sharp kick took off down the drive and away from the castle towards the safety of the dense forests. No one witnessed the death of Rory Kelly but I could only assume that the Sidhe's envoy of death had taken him into the woods and when finding the perfect Yshaped tree branch had ridden straight towards it. When the men from the estate, summoned by Cook, found his body he was still hanging there with his head wedged between the limbs, dead as the proverbial doorknob. At his feet lay the silver dressing table set belonging to Miss Amelia. The Sidhe had saved Miss Amelia's silver, but I had lost my beloved husband.

Chapter 11

The castle remained empty for six months, giving me at least a short time to grieve the loss of my beloved husband. It was then let to a wealthy exporter of agricultural goods from the north of the country. Like many wealthy families who had come over to our country from Scotland, the MacGregor families, unlike Lady Parker, were Protestant. Now mind you, I didn't hold anything against them because of their religion. It did, however, pain me to see what they regarded as Papist artifacts being removed from the chapel.

At first, it was lovely to once again hear the sound of the three MacGregor children's laughter filling the hallways of the castle, but within months, I began to worry about their excursions into the walled garden and the destruction their boisterous games caused among the delicate plantings.

It had been over six years since the last visitation of the ghoulish horse and I feared the children's play in the garden would anger the Sidhe and make them the target of the fairies' fury. When I brought Mrs. MacGregor her tea, I tried to casually warn her about the possible dangers of playing in the neglected gardens.

"Excuse me Madame, but I am concerned about the children playing in the walled garden. I'm afraid over these past few years there has been little maintenance performed on the walls and the property is littered with decaying trees that could easily fall and cause injury."

It soon became very apparent from her next remark that Mrs. MacGregor was more concerned about having the children out of the house and out of her way than for their personal safety. Slamming her tea cup down, spilling tea over the delicate lace table cloth, she said, "Mrs. O'Brien, I believe you are just the housekeeper here and if you want to remain the housekeeper here then I strongly suggest you leave the raising of my children to me. Now clean up this mess!"

Shocked by her venomous reply, I quickly lowered my head and replied, "Yes ma'am."

With that she swept out of the library, leaving me red-faced to clean up the mess left in her wake. When I returned the tray to the kitchen, old Cook was waiting and sympathetically smiled. "Don't let her upset you. She can't fire you, you know," she said, taking the tray from my still-shaking hands.

"How did you know she threatened to fire me?" I asked.

"From the look on your face and the fact she has threatened to fire me at least twice this week," she said still smiling.

"I don't see anything to smile about." I replied anxiously.

"She can't fire any of us. Her agreement with Miss Amelia states that she cannot release any of the staff or reduce our salaries without her express consent and that's something Miss Amelia will never give."

Collapsing into the nearest chair, I finally smiled and said, "Thank goodness for Miss Amelia."

Later that very evening, I ventured into the garden to check for anything which might harm the children if they were to continue to play in the garden. Because I hadn't been there for a while, I was shocked to see the trampled plants and the litter strewn around the grounds. As I was bending over picking up bits of paper and scraps and shoving them into my apron pockets, I heard a small voice whispering, "We miss Mistress Amelia. Can you bring her back?"

With my mouth gaping, I leaned forward as the fairy continued, "She would protect our home from those little people. Just look at what they've done!" squealed the smallest of the Sidhe as she pointed to the flowers lying crushed in the dirt.

The biggest of the Sidhe stepped forward and crossing her arms across her chest spewed angrily, "They are making us very cross. Just yesterday, Fiona was knocked from her perch on this very flower and nearly trampled to death by one of those wicked creatures. We won't tolerate much more of this. This is our home and we've lived here long before any of you ever came to these mountains. Our home is under attack and you must do something or we will!"

"They are not wicked creatures. They are simply children and they were only playing. They mean you no harm," I replied, trying to sound as calm as possible.

Before I could even finish speaking, they had disappeared back into the undergrowth, leaving my words hanging in the air. I knew at that very moment my words had done nothing to appease the Sidhe and something terrible was going to happen.

As I ran from the garden and past the now empty house, once home to my parents, I remembered the key. My father always kept a key to the garden's wooden door hanging from a nail by the kitchen back door. Once a year in the early spring, he would lock the door to protect the new shoots growing from the bulbs planted in the fall. Perhaps if I could find the key and lock the door then the children wouldn't be able to get in and they would be safe.

Pushing the door open and stepping over the threshold, the smell of decay and rot assailed my nose. My heart sank at the state of my parent's former immaculately clean home. Dust clung to everything and cobwebs hung like fine spun lace from every corner. I made my way as quickly as I could to the kitchen and retrieved the key before hurrying back outside as tears of loneliness and grief stung my eyes.

Wiping my tears, I crossed the lawn to the garden and checking to be sure no one had entered during my short absence, pulled the door shut and locked the garden up tight. Slipping the key safely into my apron pocket, I returned to the castle praying this would keep the children safe.

And safe they were, at least for a while. Then it happened. It was during the worst storm we had experienced since 'The Night of the Big Wind'. The ten-day period from 18th-27th February, 1903 was a very stormy one. With depressions from the Atlantic passing close-by the west coast of Ireland, the winds blew through the estate uprooting hundreds of trees, many of them crashing into the beautiful stone garden walls my father had worked so hard to create. It not only broke my heart to see the destruction of those beautiful walls caused by the storm, it also opened up more avenues of entrance to the children.

Trying to convince their mother of the danger of the fallen trees and the collapsed walls in the garden, I asked, "Madame, do you think it is advisable for the children to play in the gardens with all the damage caused by the storm?"

Once again, I was met with a stern reproach as she glared at me saying, "I can't keep them shut up in the house day and night. I need my rest and I can't rest when they are thundering up and down the stairs."

Waving her hand at me, I was dismissed and I stormed down to the kitchen. Cook took one look at my face and frowned as she placed a cup of tea on the table in front of me and said, "I see you've been speaking with Madame again."

Sighing deeply, I lifted the cup to my lips and said, "She cares more for her rest than she does the safety of her own children."

Sitting down opposite me Cook replied, "Seems like all she ever does is rest."

Old Cook's eyes suddenly took on a far-away, troubled look as she said, "I saw something very peculiar early this morning. I don't mind telling you it makes me wonder if the stories told here-about are true."

"What stories, Cook?"

"The stories of a phantom white horse that glides across the lake."

Jumping to my feet and spilling what was left of my tea, I raced from the kitchen without saying another word and followed the path to the walled garden. I could hear the children's laughter coming from within and I was relieved I had arrived in time.

Unable to enter through the door because of a collapsed wall, I lifted my skirts and began climbing over a breach in the wall. I was halfway over when I sensed the presence of something very close behind me. I could have reached out and touched him. That's how close he was. More out of anger than fear, I raised my hand and smacked him hard on his nose shouting, "Not this time! You have taken one innocent soul and I won't have you take another. They are children. They are only playing. They mean no harm to your masters. If anyone is guilty, it is their lazy mother who worries more about her precious peace and quiet than the safety of her own children."

The minute the words were out of my mouth, I regretted them. Still staring at me intently, the massive beast loudly snorted and nodding his head up and down turned to stare in the direction of the castle. Without meaning to, I had as good as signed a death warrant for Mrs. MacGregor.

Chapter 12

It wasn't long before the White Horse was to claim her. It had been a horrendous morning at the Castle. The rain had been pouring down all morning, and the children were nosily entertaining themselves by running up the steps and sliding down the curving bannister. I had been kept busy running up and down the stairs answering their mother's constant summonses and demands for me to control her children.

Just as the rain began to let up, I finally managed to entice the children into the kitchen below stairs with the promise of shortbread. They were quietly sitting around the table enjoying their biscuits and milk when I heard an almighty whooshing sound followed by a terrible crash that shook the entire castle. The children screamed loudly and immediately sought refuge under the heavy oak table, quickly followed by Cook.

Directing my attention to Cook, I yelled, "Keep the children here! I'll go see what has happened."

Racing up the stairs, I found nothing amiss in the hall but after pulling open the front door I found the cause of the terrible noise. The front portico had collapsed under the weight of a massive tree that had somehow fallen upon it. As I was surveying the damage, it suddenly occurred to me that Mrs. MacGregor hadn't even bothered to leave the sanctuary of the library. Having had enough of her disinterest in her children's welfare, I had just about made up my mind to risk my position by asking her if it hadn't occurred to her to check on her children.

Pushing open the door to the library, I began to vent my anger only to find the room empty. Where had she gone? It wasn't long before I found out.

Racing to the front door again, I peered through the broken and twisted limbs of the tree towards the lake. I was just in time to see the White Horse seem to glide across the waters of the lake, before diving down deep into its cold, still waters. I knew at that very moment that Mrs. MacGregor was dead.

Hours later, as the men from the estate were removing the tree debris, they found her. What had tempted her to leave the sanctuary of the library and venture outside, we will never know.

As soon as Mr. MacGregor returned, he immediately packed up the children and returned to their home in the north. The Sidhe had accomplished their goal and there would be no more children to intrude on their gardens. For many nights I lay awake questioning whether I had been the cause of this uncaring mother's death. My only consolation was that by confronting my fears and standing up to the White Horse, I had saved three innocent children.

Chapter 13

When the castle finally passed into new ownership in 1909, I was delighted to learn it had passed to our own Master Jamie. I hadn't seen Master Jamie since his grandmother moved to Scotland to be cared for by Lady Amelia. Master Jamie, now thirty years old, had become a successful barrister and influential Member of Parliament championing the Irish cause since his graduation from Eton.

I was walking by the lake when the motor car came roaring around the bend and up the front drive. Smoothing my hair, I quickly made my way to the front steps to greet the visitor. Motor cars were very rare in these mountains and I was more than a little surprised to see such a motor car as this coming up the drive. Coming to a halt at the bottom of the stairs, the driver jumped out over the still-closed door and pulling off his driving googles, smiled brightly and greeted me saying, "Cathleen, my very first friend and confidant at Castle Chonamara, you haven't changed a bit. You're still as lovely as ever."

Going forward to greet him, I curtsied and said, "Welcome home, Sir Jamie."

"What's with this 'Sir'?" he teased.

"It's just plain Jamie, as it has always been. Come here my silly old friend," he replied putting his arms out wide for me to step into his warm hug.

Walking arm-in-arm, we mounted the steps and walked through the doors of the home that had been a safe haven for both of us.

As we entered the front door I said, "You must be hungry and thirsty after your long trip. Shall I bring you tea in the library?"

Faking sternness, Jamie replied, "No, you may not!"

"No?" I asked confused.

Breaking into a broad grin, Jamie tucked my arm into his and propelling me towards the stairs replied, "No, my dear friend. We are going to have our tea together in the kitchen, just like we did when we were young and I had a huge crush on you."

Blushing like a schoolgirl, I allowed Jamie to lead me downstairs to the kitchen where we had indeed shared many a meal when young. After enjoying tea and doorstep sandwiches of freshly baked bread with butter and jam, Jamie began laying out his plans for the estate.

"As I'm sure you heard, I married a woman many years my junior a few years ago. My wife, shall I say, is used to the better things in life and enjoys the London society circuit. I, however, have grown weary of the constant round of parties, the outrageous bills for dressing my wife, and the entertaining costs she accumulates. I have come here, in advance, to get things in proper order so I can bring my wife here. She needs to be away from certain elements in London."

"Are there no children to keep her busy?" I asked.

"Regretfully no, perhaps had we been fortunate enough to have children she might have settled down but I suppose it wasn't in God's plan for us."

I could tell from just this brief conversation that Master Jamie longed for children and was less than happy in his marriage. This was the very last thing I would have wished for this kind and loving man.

I suddenly became fearful again, remembering the timing of Jamie's return home. I sat quietly trying to think of a way to explain to Jamie the Sidhe's curse on the castle and my concern for his safety. As though my old friend had read my mind, Jamie casually asked, "Do our little friends, the Sidhe, still live in the gardens?"

"Yes, Jamie they do, and there is more you should know about them and their curse on this estate." Jamie gave me an odd look but sat quietly waiting for my explanation.

"I found a story about the curse of the White Horse in the book your grandmother gave me that first Christmas after your father died."

Jamie leaned forward and stared into my eyes as I continued, "Your grandmother knew about the curse of the White Horse and knew he could be summoned by the Sidhe if they were displeased with anyone who lived on their sacred grounds. She knew, but she tried to keep it a secret."

Nodding, Jamie said, "I have heard the stories."

I slowly continued, "The Sidhe are powerful but there are limits to their powers. The curse only allows them to summon the horse once every seven years."

Tilting his head to the side, Jamie asked, "And why are you telling me this now?"

"Because this year marks seven years since his last appearance, and there is more. Jamie, your father didn't just fall into the lake and drown as your grandmother told you. He was forced into those waters by the White Horse. Your grandmother, Amelia and I all witnessed it."

Growing more curious, Jamie asked, "Why would grandmother lie to me and why would the horse do that? I thought he only took people who the Sidhe felt were evil. What had my father done?"

Trying to be as gentle as possible, I said, "You recently lost your mother. She was trying to spare you. As for why your father incurred the Sidhe's wrath, he was bothering the young ladies who worked on the estate."

Just nodding, Jamie replied, "Considering the way he abandoned my mother, that doesn't surprise me. But what does all this have to do with me?"

"I'm worried about you. It's been almost seven years and he could be summoned at any time, should the Sidhe desire."

Taking my hands in his, Jamie smiled and in a calm voice said, "My dearest old friend, I lived here for many years and I have always been on good terms with the Sidhe. I would never do anything to displease our little friends."

"I know you wouldn't do anything on purpose Jamie, but sometimes I think the Sidhe look for excuses to summon him. He hasn't missed coming these past forty-two years," I replied, as I began to shake uncontrollably.

That was the last we spoke of the Sidhe and the curse. Over the next few weeks, Jaime worked late into the night making changes to the estate to make it more welcoming for his young wife. He took on additional staff to get the castle up to standards and more gardeners to bring the walled garden back to its former glory. I knew without asking that the Sidhe were pleased.

It was just a month after Jamie's arrival when a caravan of vehicles of all sizes trumpeted the arrival of Lady Victoria Parker. I was determined to like my old friend's wife but I quickly found this was going to be an insurmountable task.

As soon as she was helped from her vehicle, she curled her lips up in distain at the sight of the stark, gray walls of the castle. Master Jaime was quickly at her side, eager to show off his family home. Watching her interaction with her husband, it was obvious to me that she had married my dear friend for his position and money.

I stood on the front steps with the rest of the staff to greet our new mistress but instead of uttering so much as a polite greeting to any of us, she swept past us as if she feared catching some dreadful disease. As I stood there, I wondered, 'What had Jaime seen in her? She was all looks and no substance; as cold as the ice on the lake in the dead of winter.'

Jamie stayed for another fortnight, during which time we saw very little of Lady Victoria. Jaime had arranged for horses to fill the stables again as his wife enjoyed her daily rides after breakfast, which she insisted be served to her in her bed chamber.

The night before Jamie was to leave to handle his affairs in London there was a terrible argument during their evening meal. As I was helping the wait staff, Lady Victoria casually said to her husband, "I hope you don't mind, but I've invited a few people over to stay while you're away."

Putting his fork down, Jamie raised his eyes from his plate and calmly replied, "Can this visit not wait until I return in a fortnight?"

Without hesitation, she glared at her husband saying, "No, it cannot. Besides my friends are coming to see me. They want to have a good time and frankly Jamie, they find you a bore."

I lowered my eyes, embarrassed for my dear friend, and tried to leave the room. Before I could make my exit, Jamie stopped me, "Stay right here, Cathleen. I wish you to hear my instructions to my wife so there is no misunderstanding."

I dreaded being put in the middle of this argument. Lady Victoria already resented my closeness to her husband and the thought of having her alone, without Jamie as a buffer, for a fortnight wasn't pleasant.

Looking straight at his wife, he continued, "If it is too late to stop these friends of yours from coming to my home, then they will respect it. That means, my dear wife, that there will be no abuse of my hospitality and you will behave like the respectable married woman that you are."

With that last remark, Lady Victoria rose from her chair, and picking up her still-full dinner plate, threw it directly at her husband before storming out of the room.

I slowly raised my eyes to stare open-mouthed at my old friend. Shaking his head, Jamie said, "Sit with me, Cathleen. There are things you need to know before I leave."

Dismissing the rest of the shocked staff, I sat and patiently waited for Jamie to continue.

"First, I must apologize for my wife's behavior in front of you and the staff. I'm afraid it is partially my fault. You see, I spoiled her when we first married by giving in to her every whim. All that changed six months ago when I returned home early one afternoon and found her alone in the company of a man of despicable reputation. The scandal would have ruined her and could have seriously damaged my career. This is why I have brought her to these mountains. I wanted her away from the parasites she surrounded herself with and now she arranges for them to come here to my home."

Reaching over and covering his clenched fists with my hands, I replied, "I am so sorry Jamie. Is there anything I can do?"

"There is, Cathleen. I am leaving you in charge of my home while I am gone and you are not to take any orders from my wife. I will inform my wife of my decision before I leave so there will be no question on her part about who is control. If there is inappropriate behavior, of any kind, I am giving you permission to have the offender escorted off the estate."

Lady Victoria's friends arrived just two days after Jamie left. After observing the men's familiarity with Lady Victoria, I could well understand my friend's concern regarding his wife's unbecoming behavior. I'm sure that my continuous presence when she was entertaining her friends didn't set well with her, but she made no comment. I wondered how long it would be before she would come up with a plan to escape my scrutiny. It didn't take her long.

Her plan came in the form of a fox hunt. Knowing full-well that I could not follow her on the hunt, she was finally free from my watchful eyes. Walking around the estate after their first day riding I was appalled by the destruction the riders had caused in the gardens Jamie had worked so hard to restore. I couldn't help but feel it was done deliberately to spite Jamie. I knew the Sidhe would be furious and I once again lived in fear they would summon the White Horse.

It was two days before Jamie was due back from London when Lady Victoria and two of her male friends decided to enjoy one final hunt before they left. When I heard the first of the riders coming up the drive, I hurried to the front steps with the customary tray of punch-filled stirrup cups. The two men handed their mounts over to the stable boy and smirking as they looked back in the direction, from which they came, took a cup of punch; laughing and slapping each other on the backs entered the castle. It was a few minutes before Lady Victoria came into view. She was still adjusting her clothes and patting her hair as she cantered up the drive.

I was never to find out if my suspicions about her adulterous behavior were well-founded because before I could raise the alarm, the White Horse rose from the waters of the lake reared up on its hind legs directly in front of her horse. Unable to control her spirited thoroughbred, she was unseated and thrown into the lake.   Dropping the tray of precious silver cups, I ran to the waters' edge, but she was nowhere to be seen. She must have been knocked unconscious in the fall because there were no signs of a struggle or evidence of her trying to save herself. Alerted by the sound of the tray dropping and my screams, her friends reached the lake within minutes but there was no trace of Lady Victoria, not even a ripple on the calm waters.

Lady Victoria's friends didn't even have the decency to wait for the recovery of her body from the still waters, but packed and left immediately.   Jamie had already left his London office to return home so there was no way of notifying him of the tragedy. It was to fall on me again to deliver the horrific news.

I paced the front hall the morning he was due home, listening for the sound of his motor car, hoping to catch him before he would notice the black crepe on the door. As soon as I heard his car coming up the long gravel drive, I walked slowly down the front steps to greet him. He must have known by the look on my face that something was terribly wrong.

"She's finally left me, hasn't she?" he asked as sadness filled his eyes. I hadn't realized until that very moment that Jamie still deeply loved his wife despite all she had put him through. I quickly reached out my hands to him and putting my arm around his shoulders said, "No Jamie, she didn't leave you. Come inside where we can talk more comfortably."

I managed to get Jamie into the library before telling him of his wife's death. I tried to ease his pain by lying and telling him that her behavior had been that of a lady and she had confided in me that she had missed him while he was away. Whether he believed me or not, I'll never know. I do know that Jamie was never the same after the lake claimed his young wife.

Jamie remained at the castle, never returning to his law practice in London. He spent his remaining days maintaining the estate until his money and health were both exhausted. My dear friend left this life early one bright spring morning as I sat by his bed holding his hand in mine. My heart was heavy as I watched him laid to rest in the family mausoleum beside the woman he had loved and who had caused his ruin. I was once again left alone to grieve without family or friends to comfort me.

Chapter 14

I turned sixty-two in 1917, and having spent most of my life in service here at Castle Chonamara, I was looking forward to finally retiring and living out the remainder of my years in the house my grandfather had built in the village of my birth.

The past seven years were troubling times in Ireland. The newspapers were full of tragic events, from the sinking of the Belfast-built Titanic to the devastation of the Great War. When I thought things couldn't get worse, the news reached us of the Easter Rising in Dublin in 1916, when sixteen hundred members of the militant Irish Republican Brotherhood seized several buildings in the city. Within just six days, the much stronger British forces put down the uprising and arrested the leaders, who were later executed. This political unrest was turning neighbor against neighbor, even here in this isolated area. This was nothing compared to the Spanish flu epidemic which began in July 1917 and killed nearly as many people as the Great War. The war with Germany finally ended but not before the loss of many young Irish men. It was with heavy heart that it fell to me to tell the remaining staff that Miss Amelia's son and last male heir to Castle Chonamara had been lost in one of the first battles of the war.

With no direct male heir left, it now fell to the family solicitors to search for a potential heir. With little income available, the staff was cut to the bare minimum and the estate fell into disrepair. With only one gardener left, the beautiful walled gardens became terribly overgrown. The stables, once filled with magnificent thoroughbreds, now stood empty except for the mice and rats that made their home in the hay left rotting in the empty stalls. Vines crept up the walls of the chapel, blocking what light that came through the once-magnificent stained glass windows.

With no family in residence to serve, and few visitors, I found I had more spare time to spend walking the grounds. I almost always took the same route, past the schoolhouse, my parents former home, and finally to the walled garden.

The schoolhouse, where my mother taught, now stood forlorn with a gaping hole in the roof. I often peered through the dirty and broken windows at the desks where my brothers, as young boys, had sat. Everything had been left exactly where it lay on that last day of classes before the school closed forever. The schoolbooks Lady Parker ordered those many years ago lay scattered about the desks and on the floors, covered in mildew and mold from the rain that poured in from the hole in the roof and the broken windows.

The saddest thing to me was watching the slow decay of Lady Parker's dream and my father's creation...the walled garden. Reaching into my pocket, I pulled out the heavy iron key and unlocking the massive oak door, I entered the garden. Although the garden was terribly overgrown with weeds and vines, the flowers and blooming shrubs were still magnificent. As I walked down the path towards the bench where Miss Amelia and I often sat as young girls, my dress brushed the lavender, emitting the most delicate of scents and evoking memories of happier times long past.

Closing my eyes in the warm sun, I sat on the bench as my mind wandered and remembered those memories both happy and sad. I must have dozed off until I was abruptly interrupted from my daydreaming by a quiet little voice,

"Pardon the interruption Miss, but do you know what will happen to the garden now? We have done our best to keep the flowers blooming but we can only do so much. We truly miss that gentle man who used to come every day and talk to the flowers and sing the loveliest songs."

Looking down by my feet, I saw no less than a dozen Sidhe reclining on a giant rhododendron leaf, watching me intently.

"Oh, you must mean my father. My goodness, he has been gone for many years now," I answered sadly.

"But where has he gone? Can you get him to come back?" asked the biggest of the Sidhe as he stepped forward.

"He has gone to heaven and I'm sorry to say that no one comes back from heaven."

Still persisting, the Sidhe demanded, "Heaven? What is this heaven?"

"Oh, that is a bit difficult to explain. I suppose heaven means different things to different people. When I picture heaven, I see my father surrounded by the flowers he loved with my mother by his side," I said, beginning to choke up.

"Your mother?" she persisted.

"Yes, my father followed my mother to heaven," I replied, as a tear escaped my eye and rolled down my cheek.

The Sidhe soon began to chatter excitedly among themselves in a language foreign to my ears. The largest of the fairies suddenly jumped from the leaf to a tree branch close to my face.

Reaching over and gently touching my cheek with her long pointed fingers she said in awe, "You can make rain from your eyes." Climbing down from the branch and plopping down on the bench beside me, she asked, "Are you a god?" Dangling her spindly legs over the edge of the seat she waited patiently for my reply.

Trying not to laugh at the thought of this lowly, old housekeeper being a god, I composed myself and said, "No, I am no god. These are tears of sadness, not rain drops."

Still seeming unconvinced, I dipped my finger in the rain-filled birdbath beside the bench and held it down to the Sidhe saying, "Here, taste this."

Touching his finger to mine, she placed a drop of water on his fork-like tongue.

Watching her carefully, I asked, "Now, what do you taste?"

Smacking her lips she replied, "It is rain water."

"That's right," I said before touching my finger to my tear stained cheek and offering it to the Sidhe.

"And now?" I asked.

She had no sooner put her finger to her mouth than her little face screwed up and turned as green as her tunic.

"Are you trying to poison me? What was that?" she demanded as she jumped into the birdbath and began vigorously washing out her mouth.

Fearing how alarmed the fairies were becoming and not wishing to become victim to the White Horse, I quickly explained, "No, it's not poison and will do you no harm. It is salt. Human tears contain salt, unlike rain that is pure."

Wiping her mouth on the sleeve of her tunic, she jumped back on the leaf joining the rest of the fairies. Seeming content with my answer, she asked, "Will someone come soon to tend our garden?"

Looking about the garden, I softly replied "I don't know. I hope so."

When I looked back at the leaf, the Sidhe were nowhere to be found. Shaking my head, I wondered if my mind was playing tricks on me and if I had just dozed off and dreamt the whole thing.

Days turned into weeks, until one day a large car appeared coming up the drive. As I stood on the front steps, shielding the sun from my eyes, a lady emerged from the car followed by two little girls.

The very breath was knocked from my body as she approached. She was the image of our dear departed Lady Parker. Reaching out her gloved hand to me, she said, "Hello, Cathleen. It is good to see you looking so well."

Unable to reply, the lady continued, "Don't you recognize me? I am Amelia's daughter, Anne. I know you haven't seen me since I was a child, am I that much changed?"

Forgetting all formality, I wrapped my arms around the grown woman, who had once been the impish little girl who followed me everywhere. "Of course I do Miss Anne. I was just stunned into silence by your similarity to your dear grandmother."

"Thank you, Cathleen. That is the nicest thing anyone has said to me in a very long time," she said.

Turning back to the two young girls, she brought them forward and said, "Girls, say hello to Miss Cullen. She is an old and dear

169

friend of the family who has lived here all her life."

The girls were identical twins and bore an uncanny resemblance to Miss Amelia. I couldn't help but wonder what the Sidhe would think of the arrival of two so like their beloved Amelia.

As the wind began to pick up and the sky darkened, I quickly held open the front door and said, "Shall we have some tea and catch up on the news?"

Anne hadn't gone five feet into the hall when she turned to me and gasped, "What has happened here and where is everyone?"

Staring into her shocked eyes, I replied, "Miss Anne, no one has lived here for years and since the death of Mr. Jamie and your brother, I don't ever know who owns the estate. Most of the staff had to be released because the monthly draft barely pays those who remain."

A look of shear hatred passed over Miss Anne's face before she composed herself and asked, "Would it be too much trouble to have tea in the library? It was my grandmother's favorite room and holds some of my fondest memories."

"Of course, Miss Anne, I'll see to it. Some of your dolls and games are still there in the toy box, if you think your girls would enjoy seeing them."

"Thank you, Cathleen. I'm sure they will."

Smiling, I asked, "I wish you had sent word that you were dropping by for a visit. I would have prepared something special for tea."

Looking at me with a sad smile on her face, Miss Anne replied, "I've not come just for a visit Cathleen. I have come home to stay."

Before ushering her girls into the library, Anne gazed around at the dismal state of the great hall and turned to me saying, "I'm glad to be

171

home Cathleen, and between the two of us, we will set things right if it's the last thing I ever do"

Crossing myself as I headed for the kitchen, I said a silent prayer that the Sidhe would be pleased with the return of Miss Amelia's family and end the curse forever.

Chapter 15

Returning to the library, I found Anne sitting on the floor in front of the fire playing dolls with her two daughters. Quickly rising to her feet, she took the tray from my hands and setting it on the large mahogany table she hugged me tightly and said, "It is just as I remember it. Nothing has changed in this room. It's just like when Grandmamma lived here. I could almost picture her sitting in her chair by the fire doing her lace work. How do you do it, Cathleen?" she asked.

Taking her delicate hands in my old wrinkled ones as we sat together on the settee, I replied, "With so little help, I spend what time I have keeping this room just as your dear grandmother liked it and one bedroom ready for any unexpected guests. I'm sorry the castle is so cold, but this fire and the fire in the kitchen are the only ones we light daily. But enough about me, what brings you here after all these years?"

Reaching over and pouring the tea, Anne looked over at her daughters playing so contently and said, "It's a long story and not a very happy one, and not one I care to repeat in front of the girls, so let's enjoy our tea first."

Finishing our tea, I looked at Anne and said, "Perhaps the girls would like to play in their grandmother's bedroom while we take the tray back to the kitchen?"

"That sounds like a good idea," then turning to the girls she said, "Come on girls and I'll show you where your grandmother used to play and sleep when she was your age."

Clutching their dolls, they were off in a flash bounding up the stairs ahead of their mother. I watched from the great hall below as Anne mounted the stairs as if she was carrying the weight of the world on her delicate shoulders. I knew then something was terribly wrong despite the brave face she put on.

After the girls were settled, Anne and I carried the tray back down to the kitchen and sat at the old wooden table where once a staff of over twenty had eaten their meals. Getting right to business, Anne asked, "How many do we still have working here, Cathleen?"

Looking up into her worried eyes, I said, "Only five. In addition to me, there is one gardener, one groundsman, one maid and cook. That's all the monthly draft covers and even that's with the reduction in wages."

Seeing the pain in her eyes, I quickly continued apologetically, "I'm sorry for the state of the estate, Miss Anne. We do the best we can with what we have. Thank goodness, Mr. Brown, the gardener, keeps an excellent kitchen garden or there wouldn't be enough food to eat."

Taking my trembling hands in hers, Anne replied, "That's all behind you now. Things are going to change beginning this very day."

"I don't understand Miss Anne. What can you do? We don't even know who the new owner is and even if he has been traced."

Smiling now, Anne continued, "He was found in America over a year ago and since he didn't want to move back to Ireland, or pay the inheritance taxes, he opted to sell the estate. I have owned it since then."

"But Miss Anne, then why didn't we know and pardon me for asking but why such dramatic cuts in the monthly bank drafts?"

Crinkling her brow, Anne continued, "That's because I trusted someone else to manage the estate for me and he was pocketing the money for himself."

Shocked at someone treating our Miss Anne that way I replied, "The scoundrel! I hope you fired him."

"Better than that Cathleen, I am divorcing him."

"Divorcing?"

"Yes, Cathleen, the scoundrel is my husband. I had no idea he was stealing money from my accounts until a strange woman appeared at my front door one morning after he left for his office. Seems she was his mistress and he was keeping her in style until he dumped her for a younger woman. She was so incensed she offered to accompany me to my solicitor and gave him a full sworn statement attesting to his adultery."

Outraged that someone could treat the mother of his children in such a disgusting manner, all I could reply was, "He's a fool, Anne. You're better off without him!"

Smiling and patting my hand Anne said, "Yes, I know I am now, but I must admit it came as quite a shock to me. Not as big of a shock as seeing the state of our beloved home thanks to his deceit. Unlike my marriage, this can be fixed."

And fixed it was. The very next day, Anne sent word to the local villages that the new owner of the castle would be taking on additional staff. Within a week, the castle was up to staff. Within a fortnight, the house was looking much better and the gardens were much improved.

Anne had taken to personally overseeing the work being done in the garden and often walked there with her daughters. The Sidhe had been unusually quiet during this period and I wondered how long it would be before the Sidhe made contact.

I didn't have to wait long. It was a lovely spring day, just two months after Anne's first arrival when the Sidhe made their presence known to the girls as they sat on the garden bench. I had just gone into the garden to call them in for their lunch when I noticed them leaning forward and animatedly talking to something in the flowering shrubs. I knew without a doubt the Sidhe had chosen that day to deliver one of their often ominous warnings.

178

As soon as it was apparent they had finished talking to the Sidhe, I called, "Girls, it's time for lunch."

"Coming, Miss Cathleen."

Not a word was spoken until we were sitting around the table in the kitchen where we often ate our lunch. Suddenly, Beatrice, the older of the twins looked at her mother and asked, "Mama, do you believe in fairies?"

Without hesitating, Anne replied, 'Yes dear, of course. Did you know that this castle was built on sacred ground to the Sidhe, the fairies that live in these mountains?"

Both of the girls shook their heads from side-to-side as their mother continued, "As a matter of fact, they live in the walled garden and were friends to me when I was your age."

Excitedly, both girls said together, "We know Mama!"

I looked at Anne and making eye contact with her, nodded that I had witnessed something

179

when I went to collect the girls. Anne and I exchanged worried glances, knowing this was probably not good news, as we waited for the girls to continue.

Beatrice continued, "The Sidhe talked to us. At first they were very pleasant, talking about how happy they were that we were here and their garden was being tended once again. But then they seem to become very agitated as one of them said to tell you someone is coming and this person is evil and you must be very careful."

Sensing that her daughters had been frightened, Anne remained calm and smiled as she replied, "Well, I must thank the Sidhe for their concern, but I am sure we are safe here with all of our friends around us."

Finishing their lunch, the girls were eager to return outside to play but as they were leaving, Lucy, the younger of the twins, turned at the door and asked her mother, "Can we see the White Horse, Mama?"

Trying not to let the panic Anne suddenly felt show on her face, she asked, "What white horse darling?"

"The one the Sidhe said would protect us," she replied, as she closed the kitchen door, escaping into the bright sunshine.

Both Anne and I sat quietly for a few minutes before she looked deeply into my eyes and firmly said just three words, "We must prepare."

Chapter 16

Time seems to move much faster when one gets to my age. Soon the warm days of summer faded into autumn and winter began to make itself known throughout the mountains and valleys that surrounded Castle Chonamara. It was during these first days of winter, before the deep snows came, that he arrived.

Miss Anne had received a message from her solicitor that it would be necessary for her to meet with her husband and both parties' solicitors before the marriage could be dissolved. It was arranged they would travel down to the castle so her husband could also visit with his daughters in the relaxed setting of the home, which they had now grown to love.

I had made up my mind to dislike this man, but after meeting him, I could well understand how Miss Anne had fallen so deeply in love with him. He was probably the most handsome and most charming man I had ever met. However, there was something about him that set my hair on end. I think it was the look in his eyes when he thought no one was watching him. It reminded me of the cunning old red fox that would innocently wander about the farm yard buildings waiting for a chance to get at the chickens. Yes, there was something definitely predatory about this man.

The discussions were going smoothly until it came to the matter of the financial settlement. Miss Anne had come into a vast fortune with the death of her parents and, of course, the greedy man wanted his share of this in the form of a yearly allowance for life to go away quietly. Miss Anne was not having any of this. After what seemed like hours of deadlocked discussions, the solicitors, hoping for a congenial solution, suggested they leave the couple alone to discuss the issue in private before leaving.

Had I not been busy keeping the girls out of the house and away from the often loud discussions, I would never have permitted this. We had just settled ourselves on the garden bench, when we heard the excited chatter of the Sidhe. They were holding hands and walking in a circle chatting in the strange language they often used when they didn't want me to understand them. This time something was different. The biggest of the Sidhe suddenly turned and looked at me saying, "You must go help Miss Anne. We will stay with the girls and keep them safe."

She had no sooner finished talking then I heard Miss Anne's screams for help.

Looking into the frightened eyes of the girls I said, "You stay here. I will help your mother. Don't leave the garden. The fairies will keep you safe."

I ran from the garden and almost collided with their father. He looked like a madman as he pushed me to the ground and shouted, "Where are my daughters?"

I never said a word, but my look of fear as I quickly glanced back to the door of the walled garden gave away their hiding place. Before I could get to my feet to try to stop him, he had reached the door and was trying desperately to open it. Something or someone was keeping it from opening.

Suddenly, I heard the soft sound of hoof-beats coming slowly up the mossy path behind me. He had come. Knowing now that the Sidhe had summoned the White Horse to keep Miss Anne and her daughters' safe, I turned and ran, without looking back, in the direction of Miss Anne's cries for help.

I could hear his screams as I ran out into the drive and raced up the front steps of the castle. As soon as I pushed open the front door, I could see the smoke coming from under the library door and I could hear Anne banging on the door. He had locked her in and set fire to the room.

Banging back on the door, I screamed, "Can you get to the windows, Anne?"

"No, he set the drapes on fire and it is spreading quickly," she cried.

"Stay calm, I'm going for help!" I screamed as I made for the front door. Throwing it wide open, I started down the stairs only to be confronted by the phantom white stallion pawing the ground excitedly. Blood stained his massive hooves, leaving me no doubt as to what fate had befallen Anne's evil husband.

I turned to him and choking from the smoke which was now filtering out from the hall begged, "Miss Anne is in there. She is a friend of the Sidhe, I can't open the door! Please help her!"

With that the beast climbed the stairs and entered the hall. Rearing up on his hind legs he brought his front legs crashing into the door before moving quickly into the smoke filled room.

As the door gave way under his thundering hooves, more smoke billowed out through the gaping hole making it impossible for me to see. Within seconds the smoke cleared enough for me to witness the White Horse return with Miss Anne hanging onto his long flowing mane. As soon as they were out into the hall, I grabbed Miss Anne and pulled her out through the open front door and into the fresh air. By the time we had made it to the drive, the White Horse had disappeared.

Anne turned to me and said, "Where has he gone? I want to thank him."

A sudden soft whinny made us turn and look towards the lake. Standing at the water's edge in front of the White Horse was a beautiful woman with long white hair, dressed all in white. As we watched, she pointed to the sky and said to the horse, "You have redeemed yourself and now you are free. Never again will anyone be able to summon you to do their deeds."

The killer horse had chosen of his own free will to save Anne, and then turned and looking back at us one last time glided across the still waters of the lake. We watched waiting for him to dive back down into its deep waters, where he had been condemned for displeasing the ancient gods those many years ago. But this time it was different. Whatever he had done those many years ago to displease the gods had been set to right and the beautiful goddess had come to set him free. He suddenly took one mighty leap and ascended into the clouds. When we turned back to look at the water's edge, the woman in white had disappeared. After fifty years, the curse placed on him had finally been removed and the White Horse was free to return to ride the clouds, where he always belonged.

Epilogue

Life remained peaceful at Castle Chonamara. My plans to retire and move to the cottage my grandfather built generations ago were abruptly ended when Miss Anne insisted I stay with them in the castle as a member of the family.

I pretended to protest saying it wasn't proper for the housekeeper to stay on after retirement and that people would talk, but secretly I was pleased. I had grown to love Miss Anne like the daughter I had never been fortunate enough to have and the twins kept me feeling younger than my years.

On warm days, we would often take a picnic into the garden and lying on our backs on the old blanket watch the clouds pass over our heads, hoping to catch a glimpse of the White Horse.

As for the Sidhe, they were content with knowing that the Castle would remain in the loving, capable hands of Miss Anne, and then pass to the daughters they had chosen to protect.

After fifty years, the curse on the White Horse had been lifted and the mystery of White Horse Lake had been solved. Peace had finally come to Castle Chonamara.